THE MAN
FROM U.N.C.L.E. No. 7

The Radioactive Camel Affair

*Also available in the Souvenir Press – Four Square The Man from U.N.C.L.E. series

No. 1. THE MAN FROM U.N.C.L.E.
Michael Avallone

No. 2. THE DOOMSDAY AFFAIR
Harry Whittington

No. 3. THE COPENHAGEN AFFAIR
John Oram

No. 4. THE STONE-COLD DEAD IN THE MARKET AFFAIR
John Oram

No. 5. THE FINGER IN THE SKY AFFAIR
Peter Leslie

No. 6. THE DAGGER AFFAIR
David McDaniel

THE MAN
FROM U.N.C.L.E. No. 7

The Radioactive Camel Affair

PETER LESLIE

Based on the MGM television series
The Man from U.N.C.L.E.

Published by Souvenir Press Ltd.
in association with
The New English Library Ltd.

Conditions of Sale: This book shall not, without the written consent of the Publishers first given, be lent, re-sold, hired out or otherwise disposed of by way of trade in any form of binding or cover other than that in which it is published.

Copyright ©, 1966, by Metro-Goldwyn-Mayer, Inc.

All rights reserved

✱

First published in Great Britain by Souvenir Press Ltd., 95 Mortimer Street, London, W. 1, in association with The New English Library Ltd., Barnard's Inn, Holborn, London, E. C. 1. in July 1966

Four Square Books are published by The New English Library Limited, from Barnard's Inn, Holborn, London, E.C.1. Made and printed in Great Britain by C. Nicholls & Company Ltd.

THE RADIOACTIVE
CAMEL AFFAIR

CHAPTER ONE

SECRET FREIGHT

NAPOLEON SOLO shielded his eyes against the blazing sun. Under the folds of his burnous, the heavy Mauser automatic had worn a sore place on his hip and he shifted the belt supporting its makeshift holster. Beneath his aching thighs, the dromedary lurched and swayed, picking its way over the shale slanting up to a massive limestone bluff a thousand feet above them.

The caravan was a big one – a long line of camels, horses, men and women, some mounted and some on foot, snaking its way for almost a mile across the desolate plateau. It had been nearly five hours since they struggled up the steep valley from the last village; five hours of torment for Solo as the sun rose giddily in the sky and the caravan as inexorably climbed towards the southwest, through barren foothills pockmarked with patches of thin scrub, along a ridge of rock and sand where nothing but thorn bushes broke the monotony of the scorched terrain, and now across this bleak upland slope beyond which – he fervently hoped – their path would at last tilt downwards again.

Solo eased the belt once more, scanning the plateau with aching eyes. Below and behind them, the dead land dropped away in parallel ridges of ochre and gamboge. Above, some geological unconformity had placed a thin vein of richer rock between the weathered shale and the limestone above it, and here a streak of brownish vegetation daubed the foot of the bluff. A few hundred yards farther on, the line of stunted bushes followed the strata as they dipped towards a fault gashing in the rock face. It was in the direction of the wedge of cobalt sky marking this defile that the head of the caravan was now moving.

Once between the towering walls of the cleft, the relief from the sun's assault was immediate. It was still stiflingly hot in the shadowy gorge, but in contrast to the hammering of the direct rays, the respite seemed as refreshing as a cool shower.

Solo moistened his lips with lukewarm water from a padded bottle slung over his shoulder, reflecting wryly that it was less than a week since he had sipped scotch-on-the-rocks under the striped awning of his hotel room balcony in Khartoum.

It was like a dream from another age. In the interim he had stained his skin, bribed a policeman, been secretly taken to the caravan rendezvous forty miles south of the city, and ridden painfully half across the Sudan. They had skirted the blistering Nubian Desert, crossed the White Nile, traversed the southern fringe of the Sahara, and were now laboriously making their way across the gaunt massif which separated the province of Kordofan from Southwest Sudan. Tomorrow they were due at Wadi Elmira.

After the open wastes of the plateau, the rock walls of the pass seemed to amplify the noises of the caravan: the beasts' stony footfalls, the creaking and jingling of pack stays and harness, an occasional guttural murmur of conversation in front or behind. All these sounded unnaturally loud to Solo as they wound slowly through the defile. For the fortieth time he wondered if his disguise, his reasons for being there, his knowledge of nomad customs and of Arabic, would again aid him when they made camp for the night.

The caravan was mixed. There were ivory merchants and dealers in ostrich feathers, traders leading pack camels loaded with bales of merchandise destined for Bahr el Ghazal and the Central African Republic, and the usual supernumeraries – individual travellers and nomads who had tagged on for the ride. For this was dangerous country: the Africans of the south were in open revolt against the ruling arabs from the north, and small isolated groups could easily fall victim to one of the guerilla bands or even to over-zealous arab troops on a police operation.

The largest single group was a collection of pilgrims on their way to some obscure shrine in Equatoria, and it was as one of these people that Solo had disguised himself. The pilgrims, however, were leaving the main body of the caravan and heading south as soon as they left Wadi Elmira. It was vital for Solo to acquire certain information before this happened.

As he rode out of the gorge into the full glare of the sun, he saw with relief that the trail now led downwards across a stretch of broken country dotted with huge limestone boulders. The sun was beginning to sink in the brassy bowl of the sky; the furnace-like quality of the early afternoon was now tempered with an occasional puff of hot, dry wind, which blew from the southwestern side of the massif.

Two hours later they halted for the night.

The caravan boasted entertainers and as the western sky drained through vermilion to a limpid green above the rim of the *wadi* on whose dried up river bed they were camped, plaintive quarter-tones of arab strings and pipes rose into the rapidly cooling air. Sitting, like most of the pilgrims, in the outer rank of squatting figures around the fires, Solo dipped his fingers into the aromatic mess which filled the bowl on his lap and silently watched tumblers and acrobats as he ate. Soon, however, it was time for the girl to perform – and as he had feared, for this had happened on the two previous nights, she sought him out again, apparently performing the greater part of her act for his exclusive benefit...

She was a belly dancer. Not a very good one, possibly – but the brown body with its eloquent hips spoke as if she had tossed a card with her telephone number on it into Solo's lap. Her name was Yemanja, probably, Solo thought, of mixed Arab and Negro parentage. Certainly the name was of Yoruba origin, and while she had the nubile figure and high-bridged nose of most Mohammedan women, the full-lipped mouth and smouldering eyes were pure African. She was the property of Ahmed, the camel-master in charge of the caravan, a sullen and muscular man from the Nile Delta whose glowering regard had already been drawn towards Solo far too often for his liking. "All I need," Solo thought grimly, "is to get involved in a punch-up with a jealous boyfriend!"

Desperate as he was to avoid attention of any kind, he let out his breath in a long sigh of relief when at last the dance was over and Yemanja, with a final flash of her eyes, was gone. The girl seemed to have taken a fancy to him and was making a nightly attempt to entice him. . . . He shrugged mentally, determined to keep well clear of her, as a group dance started on the far side of the firelit circle.

Solo watched for a while. Then, as the music and dancing grew wilder and the fires burned lower, he slipped unobtrusively away, to erect his bivouac near his tethered beast. He could see here and there on the perimeter of the camp isolated groups of figures similarly engaged.

The night was cold. They had come down a long way from the pass but the valley was still more than six thousand feet above sea level. He rolled himself in his striped blanket and eased into the low tent.

Ten minutes later he was crouched under the coverings with his lips against the grille which pierced one side of a flat bakelite box about the size of a cigarette packet. He thumbed a button on top of the instrument, and a faint, barely discernible whine quivered on the cool air.

Solo turned a knurled wheel set flush with the back of the box and the whining noise increased slightly. He spun the wheel the other way; the whine faded, vanished momentarily, and then swelled again. Patiently, he experimented until he had located the null-point, the setting where the noise was tuned right out. Then he spoke very softly into the grille.

"Solo calling Station K," he breathed. "Solo calling Station K. If you receive me do not – repeat, do *not* answer. Give me the signal specified in Schedule T . . ."

He paused. After a moment, the tiny transmitter-receiver emitted three very faint pips in rapid succession.

Solo spoke again. "Fine," he said. "Now listen carefully. I dare not repeat anything and I can only talk for a moment. . . . Transmit this message in Code Three to U.N.C.L.E. headquarters in New York, top priority. Message begins. Attention Waverly. Stop. Have located post office. Stop. Hope to identify package and consignee's address tomorrow before distribution of mail. Stop. Advise Kuryakin – repeat, Kuryakin. Stop. Signed Solo. Message ends . . . Please acknowledge on Schedule T."

The receiver emitted a single prolonged bleep.

"Okay," Solo whispered. "Please listen again tomorrow

between twenty-one hundred hours and twenty-two-thirty. Over and out."

He stowed the instrument in a pouch under his burnous and rolled himself into his blanket again. The Mauser lay conveniently within reach, underneath the roll of clothes and extra bedding serving him as a pillow. . . .

In a large tent with a fly-sheet on the far side of the circle of dying fires, a tall man in dark robes leaned back from an open suitcase which was full of complicated electronic equipment. His acquiline features creased into a scowl at once petulant and menacing.

"Somebody in this caravan is using a radio transmitter," he said softly. "It's on quite a different wavelength to ours – but there's no doubt about it." He glanced down at the tuners and dials in the suitcase as though for confirmation.

"Can you get a – fix, is it? – on the transmitter with this machine?" his companion asked.

The tall man looked at him for a second. Although he was also dressed in Arab robes, the other man was unmistakably an African. "No, Colonel," the tall man said evenly; "unfortunately we cannot. We have the means to establish its existence – but there's nothing here that could locate it. Nevertheless, this proves there may be spies about. They must be identified and . . . taken care of. Perhaps you would be good enough to send Ahmed to me. In the meantime, we shall see if we can pick up anything more definite."

He turned back to the suitcase as the Nubian left the tent, and began experimentally turning the milled control wheels.

But this time there was no response. Napoleon Solo was asleep. Tomorrow he had a hard day's work before him. He knew that somewhere in the caravan, concealed among the bales of merchandise, traders' samples, rolls of bedding or folded tents, there was a small but extremely heavy canister of solid lead. Nestling in a cavity within it was a quantity of Uranium 235.

Before they reached Wadi Elmira and the caravan split into two parts, Solo had to locate that canister and find out who was carrying it. . . .

CHAPTER TWO

MR WAVERLY SETS THE SCENE

"URANIUM 235!" Napoleon Solo had exclaimed in New York two weeks previously. "But that's incredible. . . . I mean, Uranium 235 on a *camel*!"

The tall, lean man who gazed out of the room's solitary window at the United Nations building spoke without turning round. "It may sound so at first," he said. "But can you think of a better way, a more inconspicuous way, of taking it into the heart of Africa?"

"Well, no . . . I guess not. But who needs Uranium 235 in the middle of Africa, Mr Waverly?"

Alexander Waverly swung round and faced his Chief Enforcement Officer. His lined face was very grave. "Somebody does, Mr Solo," he said soberly. "Somebody does. And, given that fact, for what reason could they possibly want this particularly fissile isotope of Uranium? – in Africa or anywhere else?"

"Other than for research, the only positive use for Uranium 235 that I know is as part of an H-bomb," returned Solo.

"Precisely. It's the indispensible ingredient of a thermonuclear device," Waverly said pedantically.

"But in Africa? . . . What part of Africa?"

"That we do not know. But we must find out – at once."

"Okay. But I still don't see . . . I mean, there are no nuclear powers *in* Africa. Ourselves, Russia, China, Britain, France – we're the only countries that have the bomb. India, Italy and one or two others are coming along. But they haven't got it yet. And none of them are in Africa."

"Granted."

"Then what country could possibly – ?"

"I didn't say it was a country," Waverly interrupted – and he placed a peculiar emphasis on the last word.

Solo whistled softly. "You mean THRUSH is attempting to become the sixth nuclear power – somewhere in Africa?"

"It's a possibility we have to take very seriously indeed."

"What exactly do we know?"

Waverly crossed to the enormous teak desk that filled the centre of the large room. "You'd better come down to Communications, and I'll fill you in on what we have," he said. "Is Mr Kuryakin here yet?"

"Should be arriving any moment," Solo said, glancing at his wrist watch.

"Good. Then we can wait for him there." He pressed a button on a raised platen which projected from the surface of the desk and moved towards the door.

Three floors below, Illya Nickovetch Kuryakin paid off his cab and went into Del Floria's tailor shop, premises occupying the ground floor of a decaying brownstone building in the middle of a seedy row; this was completed at its north end by a public garage and at the south by a three-storey whitestone whose two lower floors comprised an exclusive "key-club" restaurant. However, on the top floor, above the club, a sedate suite of offices was labelled with the letters U.N.C.L.E.

A curious visitor might have imagined that the rather ordinary workers engaged in these offices were dealing with the routine business of a charity project or were the headquarters of a fund foundation. In fact, the entire block was owned by U.N.C.L.E. – the United Network Command for Law and Enforcement. The employees of the garage, the tenants of the crumbling brownstones, indeed most of the key-club patrons, were all on the organization's payroll. The Command's actual headquarters – like a kernel within a nut – was sheathed within the shell of the four old buildings in the middle of the block. Here were three floors of an ultra-modern office building, a complex steel maze of corridors and suites housing personnel of many races, creeds and colours, as well as a mass of the most advanced computers, filing and communications systems in the world. The enclave resembled most other modern buildings except in two respects: apart from the one window looking across the East River from Alexander Waverly's office, it had no direct communication whatever with the world outside; and there were no staircases. Four elevators handled the vertical traffic – and these communicated with the four secret entrances to the U.N.C.L.E. headquarters.

Strangers and visitors, if ever invited, were brought in via an elevator from the back of the offices on the top floor of the whitestone building. Normal personnel drove their cars to the garage and entered through the men's and women's washrooms there. A third entrance – more often in truth used as an exit! – was provided by an underwater channel carved through from the river to the building's basement. And the fourth means of entry – restricted to the Enforcement Agents, the elite of the Command's operational staff – was through Del Floria's shop.

Illya Kuryakin entered the shop now. He was in a hurry, his thin blond hair blown forward over his high forehead, for Waverly's summons had been unexpected and he had been sleeping late in his small and untidy bachelor apartment on the other side of town.

"Mr Kuryakin!" Del Floria exclaimed, coming from behind the steam of his pressing machine. "Always in a rush! So maybe you let me at least press that jacket for you today? Truly, you don't look so elegant in those clothes . . ." He gazed critically at Illya's black rollneck sweater, corduroy trousers and crumpled tweed jacket.

"Sorry, Del," Kuryakin smiled. "Urgent today. Mr Waverly is waiting for me. Next time, perhaps." He strode through and entered the third fitting cubicle at the rear of the shop.

"Rush, rush, rush. Always in a tearing hurry," the old man grumbled. "This modern world. . . . I don't know." He shook his head, sighed, shrugged resignedly, and pressed a button at the side of his machine. Inside the booth, Kuryakin drew the curtain, twisted the coat-hook on the back wall, and pushed. The cubicle wall swung soundlessly outwards and he walked into a well-appointed foyer.

This was Admissions – the central point to which elevators and passages from all four entrances led. There was rumoured to be a fifth entrance, known only to Alexander Waverly and his four colleagues, who between them comprised U.N.C.L.E.'s highest echelon: the Policy Department of Section One. But nobody had ever discovered where it was.

The girl on duty was a former West Indian beauty queen. She had watched Kuryakin's entrance through Del Floria's shop on one of the four closed-circuit television monitors set above her desk. Now, as he came through the door and crossed the foyer towards her desk, she looked at him approvingly through enormous, slumbrous eyes.

"Good morning, Mr Kuryakin," she said in her deep voice. "I think Mr Waverly's expecting you. Would you please join him and Mr Solo in Communications?"

Although he now worked for an international organization, Illya had been born in Russia. And he still retained much of his Slav imperturbability. For all the expression that showed on his smooth, bland face, the girl's curvaceous figure and pliant waist, even the tempting curve of her mouth, might have been carved from stone.

"Good morning, Viola," he said politely. "I am afraid I may be a few minutes late. If you would kindly pin on my badge, I'll go straight up."

The girl sighed. Like many of the female personnel at the Command's headquarters, she found Kuryakin's serene detachment a constant challenge to her femininity. She was sure that once those sensitive features could be persuaded to relax a little and to warm up... Still... she sighed again and reached into the top right-hand drawer of her desk, taking out a small white badge which she pinned lingeringly on his lapel. (The badges were another aspect of security. A red one admitted the wearer only to the ground floor, where day to day routine operations were completed. A yellow badge permitted entry to the ground and second floors – where the organization's communications centre was located. And a white one was reserved for those who rated admission to the Policy and Operations Sections on the third. A chemical on the receptionist's fingertips activated the badge as it was pinned in place, and anyone mounting to a floor higher than his badge allowed automatically tripped a complex alarm system which flashed red lights on every desk in the building, sliding steel doors across the passages to trap the intruder.)

Illya found Waverly and Solo in a small room on the second floor lined with grey filing cabinets, a projector and screen set up in one corner. Pilot lights gleamed from a complicated tape deck housed in a recess beside the door. There was a single buff cardboard folder on the table in the middle of the room.

A lock of crisp, dark hair had fallen forward over Solo's alert face, and there was a troubled look in his eyes.

"Ah, Mr Kuryakin." Waverly nodded in greeting. "There is work to be done. I think it will save questions afterwards if I take this thing right from the beginning." He crossed to a door set between two banks of steel cabinets and threw it open. "If you would be so kind as to join us, gentlemen. . . ."

A plump army officer with a bald head and a hooked nose came into the room, followed by a tall, thin man with a crewcut and rimless glasses.

"General Powers from the Pentagon; Mr Forster from the Central Intelligence Agency." Waverly introduced them with a wave of his hand. "Mr Solo and Mr Kuryakin are our two top Enforcement Officers."

They sat down around the table and Waverly dragged a sandblasted briar pipe from the pocket of his baggy jacket. "Perhaps you'd like to acquaint these gentlemen with your side of the affair, Mr Forster," he said, ramming tobacco into the bowl from an oilskin pouch.

The CIA man cleared his throat. "By all means. Not much to tell, really. Just that there's been a gradual series of thefts of Uranium 235."

"Gradual?"

"Over the past three years. We hadn't paid all that much attention until one of our computers came up with a rundown a couple of months back. We realized then that the operation method in each case was identical."

"I should have thought even one theft of 235 merited a great deal of attention," Waverly put in drily.

"Oh, sure. Every one was a big deal. On file, top priority, kept very secret – and all hell breaking loose to try and get the stuff back and identify the thieves."

"Then . . . ?"

"What I mean is, *we* – the CIA – hadn't paid all that attention until we realized the thing followed an international pattern."

"*Inter*national?" Illya echoed.

"Sure. They lifted the stuff from Hanford, from Clinton; from Calder Hall in England and Dounreay in Scotland; from Chatillon, near Paris, France; and from Magnitogorsk – "

"From Russia!" Solo exclaimed. "If it *is* a THRUSH job, surely that was very foolish of them?"

"You mean tipping us off that it wasn't the other side? Could always have been the Chinese. Or even the Soviets raiding their own places as a blind."

"Yes, I suppose so. What kind of amounts were involved?"

"Individually, pretty small. But if you add the lot together it amounts to quite a packet. That's why we called in your boys when we figured it was a planned series by persons unknown."

"You're sure it's not the Soviets?" Illya asked.

"Absolutely. Why would they bother? They make more than we do."

"True. And none of it has been recovered?"

"Not an ounce. They were clever operations alright. Every one an inside job; not a man connected with the thefts identified."

"With the security set-up surrounding nuclear physics, I should have thought that was impossible."

The CIA man shrugged. "Nothing's impossible. It happened. The point is – who took it, and why?"

"Perhaps General Powers could enlighten us at least on the latter point," Waverly intervened. "He's the thermonuclear expert."

Powers twitched podgy shoulders to re-settle his immaculately cut olive-drab jacket. In contrast to the clipped Bostonian of Forster and the mid-Atlantic accents of Solo and Illya, his voice was harsh and twangy with the intonation of the middle-west. "Yeah. Well, I guess you gentlemen have gotten used to the fact that whoever took this U-ranium 235 took it for one purpose and one purpose only: to use in the manufacture of thermonuclear bombs."

Waverly had for some minutes been tamping the tobacco down into the bowl of his pipe with the forefinger of his right hand. Now he laid the pipe down on the table and leaned forward. "That was the obvious conclusion," he said. "And since nations are very touchy on matters of their own defence – and since, furthermore, there were international ramifications to this affair – our friends at the CIA thought it best to hand the baby over to us, as we are ourselves an international organization. If, on the other hand, it is not some power-hungry nation at work but THRUSH up to its evil tricks again – then again we know more about their *modus operandi* than anyone else ...."

"Quite. Well, the first thing we have to consider," General Powers resumed, "is how this stolen material can be used. First of all, we can rule out the crude atom bomb: that's kid stuff now. Secondly, I figure we can forget the cobalt bomb. Most everybody's too goddamned scared to touch it. And that leaves us with the conventional thermonuclear fusion bomb.... Now I guess you gentlemen are familiar with the principal of this device?" He looked around the circle of attentive faces and continued before anyone could speak: "As you are probably aware, there are three separate explosions involved – or more properly four, if you count the original detonator. The detonator sets off a charge of conventional explosive which hurls together two quantities of fissile material totalling more than that substance's critical mass. This initiates a chain reaction which produces a fission explosion – and it is only in the immense heat generated by this that the fusion process involving the bomb's main constituents can take place."

"You mean an H-bomb has to be triggered off by a small A-bomb explosion inside it?" Solo asked.

"Er – yes. If you want to put it like that. Now the odd thing is," Powers continued, "that the light elements required for the fusion reaction – that is the main explosive substances in an – er – H-bomb – can be acquired by any country or organization with any resources. What stops every country in the world going nuclear is the difficulty and expense of obtaining the fissile material involved in the initial atom-bomb blast."

"And that is – Uranium 235?"

"Or Plutonium 239. Precisely."

"So that whoever has this stolen Uranium 235 – provided they can command reasonable resources – could be setting up a plant and manufacturing H-bombs in some secret place . . . say, somewhere in Africa?"

"Certainly. Mind you, 'reasonable' resources are pretty astronomic by ordinary standards. But if they had the means, and a sufficiently isolated place, and the labour, and some way of getting equipment and material there; if they had all these things – and they're big enough 'ifs' at that, gentlemen! – then I guess it could be done."

"They couldn't make it without the Uranium 235?"

"Definitely not. Not unless funds were virtually unlimited and they'd been working on it for years. You see, first of all you have to get your Uranium ores. Then you have to extract and refine pure Uranium. Then the 235 isotope has to be separated from the natural Uranium in a nuclear reactor – and the yield is minimal: only decimal seven of one per cent. When you add to this the cost of the raw material, the cost of the plant, the time, the cost of the immensely thick shielding needed – "

"Quite, quite," Waverly interrupted. "I think you've made your point, General."

"I mean, sure, they could get their deuterium, their heavy hydrogen, their cadmium and their graphite moderators easy enough; they could build themselves a reactor – "

"Why Uranium 235, though?" Illya put in, trying to stop the General's enthusiastic description. "I thought Plutonium was preferred nowadays because the yield from Uranium was so much greater."

"Why bother when you're stealing it anyway?" Forster said laconically. "I guess maybe security's even tougher on Plutonium – or perhaps the guy masterminding the deal has some reason for preferring the other isotope."

"Yes, well, the point is, it's 235 that's been stolen and accumulated," Waverly said hurriedly. "And what we have to do is track it down and find out where it's going – and why." He had pulled another pipe from his pocket, a short-stemmed cherrywood, and was absentmindedly filling it. The briar lay unsmoked on the table. He rose abruptly to his feet and moved to the projector.

"If I may hold the floor for a moment, gentlemen," he said, "I will tell you the little we have been able to find out so far..."

CHAPTER THREE

A MESSAGE FROM THE DEAD

"Soon after the CIA and the Pentagon had referred this matter to us," Waverly had said oracularly, switching on the projector and standing like a lecturer by the bright rectangle of blank screen, "we had a break: MI5 in Britain reported a further theft of 235 – from Aldermaston this time. But on this occasion they had a line on the culprit. You remember Martens?"

"The physicist who went over to the Communists while he was on holiday in Czechoslovakia last month?" Illya said.

"That's the one. Apparently his nerve broke after he'd taken the stuff and he tried to seek asylum in Prague. But the Reds weren't having any and they handed him back – which seems to confirm they had nothing to do with the theft. Anyway, he comes up for trial in two or three weeks' time – but in the meantime his wife had found something out and contacted Scotland Yard. So when Martens was handed over, they had discovered the theft and knew what questions to ask. He only knew one contact, of course, but it was a start. They didn't recover the isotope but they were able to trace it to Marseilles."

"And the contact?" Solo asked.

"Unfortunately he met with an accident," Waverly replied drily. "Apparently he fell under a train . . ."

"That's typical THRUSH stuff. Stop them talking at all costs."

"Yes. Anyway, with the information we received from Interpol, we felt we had enough to start something. I sent Devananda Anand to Marseilles."

Forster, the CIA man, cleared his throat again. "You've had reports from him?" he asked eagerly. "He's on to something?"

"We've had . . . messages. No reports as such. A piece of film, a tape, a piece of paper. Obviously they were on to Anand, close behind – and presumably he was too closely watched to use any of the normal channels and report properly." Waverly started the projector. "Anand's cover was as a newsman seeking colourful feature material for a syndicate. He managed to airmail one small can of 8 mm colour stock purporting to be samples of the kind of pictures he was able to offer. Of course it's in a kind of visual code, in case it fell into the wrong hands."

Letters and figures whirled across the small screen. Then suddenly it erupted into a blaze of light and colour. A line of camels walked slowly in silhouette across a skyline of ridged dunes. The film cut abruptly to a close-up of a revolving postcard stand outside a tourist souvenir shop. The gaudy photographs spun slowly to a halt and the camera tracked in and picked up a card which showed a harbour scene against an improbable blue sky. Another cut was followed by a second view of camels, this time against a background of stormclouds and minarets. Next came a street scene – the conventional casbah shot: a crowded alleyway with brightly coloured stalls at each side and a throng of veiled women and gesticulating men in robes. The camera panned along one side of the street and held a booth displaying arab hardware – row upon row of copper pans, pots, beakers and other containers. Then came the camels once more: a medium close-up of arabs loading bales of merchandise on to three dromedaries. This scene was double-exposed at the end, the later shot emerging as a crossroads outside a mosque. Under a purplish, dusky sky a signpost stood in the foreground. On it was written in French, English and Arabic *Bahr El Gazzara* – 235 *Km*. A final shot showed camels yet again: a long caravan winding into a picture-book sunset. Then the screen went blank.

Waverly switched off the projector. "That seems fairly clear to me," he said. "What do you make of it, Mr Solo?"

"Camels," Solo said with a grin. "They come over loud and clear, don't they? Camels going to wherever that harbour on the postcard was – "

"We've identified it. It's Alexandria."

"Camels on their way to Alexandria, then. I'm not too sure if the casbah street scene is significant, but . . . "

"The hardware shop is, surely?" Illya interjected. "All

those metal vessels ... couldn't they imply *canisters*? Remember it was followed by a shot of camels being loaded."

"Yes – I guess you're right at that! With the signpost with the figures 235 just in case we missed the point. I shouldn't think the place it pointed at was relevant.... So we have camels loaded with a canister or canisters of Uranium 235 on their way to Alexandria. That figures. But on their way to Alexandria from where ... ?"

"The film was taken in Casablanca," Waverly said. "Anand sent a tape commentary to go with it by another plane. Most of it's just cover stuff, of course, but there's a message there as well." He crossed the room and switched on the recorder in the recess by the door.

"*As I stand in the native quarter of this age-old city – the international melting pot where east meets west and plot a coup d'etat – it is difficult to resist a twinge of alarm at the evidence of the twentieth century's encroachment on centuries of tradition ...*" The soft Indian voice with its characteristically rolled r's filled the room.

"*... Listening to the cry of the muezzin as it wavers at dusk across the domed roofs and mud walls of the old town –* "

Waverly had switched the machine off. "That's a pre-arranged cue," he said. "From the word 'wavers' onwards, it's a message for me." He ran the tape back a couple of revolutions and pressed the plunger again.

"*... muezzin as it wavers at dusk across the domed roofs and mud walls of the old town, one cannot help wondering where this modern age, this nuclear era, is leading Africa. Habib Tufik has run a coffee shop in Casablanca for forty years – and if anyone has a finger on the pulse of North Africa, he has. But the things he told me of the impact of progress on this historic town are disquieting. The angular lines of this ferro-concrete block of flats are anything but wavering, for example, and yet despite their convenience, the arabs shun –* "

"That's all," Waverly said, switching the machine off. "The rest's all travelogue guff for cover. The message ended at 'anything but wavering'. So we have camels loaded with the stolen 235 leaving Casablanca for Alexandria – and we have Mr Habib Tufik and his coffee shop as a contact with disquieting news. The only other message I have is this." He picked up the folder from the table. In it was a single piece of paper: a buff telegram form. He looked at it for a moment and then handed it to each of them in turn.

"It was handed in at the main post office in Casablanca and sent, in clear, to his cover address yesterday afternoon," Waverly said. "They must have been pretty hard on his heels." The strips of teletyped lettering spelled out:

CASABLANCA FRA212 HEURE DE DEPOT 1415 DATE DE DEPOT 21/5 MOTS 8

ELT WAVERLY COLORPIX NEW YORK

FLYING EASTWARDS TOMORROW REGARDS - ANAND

"Does that mean he's leaving today for Alexandria?" Forster asked, handing the telegram back to Waverly.

"No. If he was taking a plane to follow up something, he'd never have bothered to cable me – especially in clear. He'd simply have reported his arrival when he got there. Flying also means birds – and birds imply THRUSH to me. I think he was trying to tip us off that the latest consignment of 235, the canister stolen from Aldermaston, is due to leave Casablanca for Alexandria today."

"You're speaking of him in the past tense," Solo said suddenly, accusingly. The gentle-voiced Indian agent was a particular friend of his.

Waverly coughed. "I'm afraid so," he said gruffly. "They must have caught up with him soon after he sent the telegram. . . . His body was found in an alley in the casbah this morning. He'd been beaten and robbed – and then knifed. Or so the local police say . . . "

Solo's breath hissed between his teeth. "You're letting me handle this myself, of course," he said. It was a statement rather than a question.

"You and Mr Kuryakin together, yes."

"When do we leave?"

"Now."

"Okay, I'll get back to my apartment and – "

"I said *now*, Mr Solo."

"You mean this instant? Right away? But . . . "

"What about clothes and things?" Illya asked.

"That will be taken care of. There are THRUSH agents everywhere. I don't want you two seen outside this building again – you may be watched; you may be picked up, trailed. Anything might tip them off ... Go to the armoury and draw your weapons. Stores and Equipment already have the necessary clothes, documents, cover stories and so on. You will leave by the East River entrance in ... " he consulted his watch ". . . in fifty-one minutes precisely. The launch will take you to a navy carrier anchored out in the Sound. General Powers has arranged with the Navy Department for a jet to take you to Nice. From there you can adopt your covers and fly to Casablanca on a commercial airline."

"And keep in touch, gentlemen, please," Powers said heavily. "Any shift – any prospective shift – in the balance of nuclear power is vital, absolutely vital information for our strategic planners."

"Don't forget, too, that the location of the destination of this material's not the only thing," Forster said. "Apart from Martens, every single man responsible for those thefts is still working undercover, undetected, in the nuclear plants where they occurred. We'll have to have their names, please."

Solo smiled ruefully. "Any little commissions you'd like me to undertake for you?" he asked. "Some halva, perhaps? A nice rug? ... No? Oh, well – Mr Habib Tufik in Casablanca, here we come! Who's for coffee ... ?"

CHAPTER FOUR

NIGHT IN CASABLANCA

AND so Napoleon Solo and Illya Kuryakin had found themselves – thirteen days before Solo sent his message from the camp in the uplands of southern Sudan – seeking a coffee shop in Casablanca.

Contrary to all expectations, it was raining – a sullen, relentless downpour, slanting under pressure from a westerly wind, which bounced ankle-high off the shining runways, overflowed the gutters of the old town, and cascaded from flapping awnings over the deserted sidewalks.

They had gathered from the build-up on Devananda Anand's posthumous tape that Habib Tufik's coffee shop might be something of a tourist attraction, the kind of place known to every hotel porter and cab driver in the city. But nobody in their hotel had ever heard of it, it rated no mention in the local guide, and the first three taxis they hired had to confess themselves beaten after driving – it seemed to Illya and Solo – half way around Morocco. At last Solo decided to try asking coffee wholesalers: presumably if Habib Tufik ran a coffee shop, he had to obtain supplies from somewhere. And at their second port of call, they had finally managed to get the address.

By the time they had found a fourth taxicab, and the driver had found his way to the narrow alleyway in the casbah where the place was alleged to be, it was well after dark.

"I can go no further, Messieurs," the driver said, looking at them curiously. "The road becomes too narrow. You will find the place, I think, up there on the left, in a courtyard.... It is not my business to ask, but ... " He paused.

"Yes?"

The cabbie shrugged. "Nothing. It is of no importance." He slammed the big Chevrolet into reverse and began backing towards an intersection. "Just keep your hands on your wallets, that's all!" he yelled as the car drew slowly away from them.

Solo glanced at Illya and raised an eyebrow. "A word to the wise, eh?" he said. "Let's go."

Rain was still pelting down, streaming over the alleyway which twisted uphill between tall, blank facades. The gutters, choked every few yards with refuse, formed a series of dams which had spread out and flooded the glistening cobbles, and the agents' footsteps, as they splashed their way towards a dim street light at a bend in the road, were almost drowned in the loud gurgling of running water.

Beneath the lamp, an archway led to a paved court with half a dozen houses on each side. Faintly above the drumming of the rain they could hear an outdated rock-and-roll number warring with Moorish music.

Habib Tufik's coffee-shop was at the far end of the cul-de-sac. They pushed open a wrought-iron gate set in the crumbling wall, walked down a passageway, and went in through a heavy, iron-studded door. Heat and light and noise enveloped them. The low-ceilinged, smoke-filled room was jammed with men of a dozen different nationalities. They were crouched over low tables around the walls, crowded around a bar and standing in gesticulating groups. Above the babble of voices, the rock record blared from a gaudy juke-box in one corner.

The level of conversation dropped abruptly as Solo and Illya entered, but it resumed its former pitch by the time they pushed their way to the bar. From behind the handles of an Italian espresso machine labelled *Funzione senza vapore*, a hard-faced man in his shirt-sleeves looked at them enquiringly. Judging from the general condition of a party of French sailors who shouted beside them, the place served stronger drinks than coffee.

"Cognac," Solo said brusquely, mopping his drenched hair with a handkerchief and shaking the rain from his waterproof. "Two large ones."

"*Bien, M'sieu.*"

"The proprietor is here this evening?" Solo asked conversationally, after they had surveyed the brawling crowd for a few minutes in silence. There appeared to be no waiters, the ugly-looking customers shouldering their way through the press and shouting their orders across the bar whenever they needed fresh supplies. And certainly there was nobody who looked as though he might be the owner.

"*M'sieu?*"

"Monsieur Tufik," Solo said in French. "He is here tonight?"

The hard-faced barman regarded him levelly. "But of course. He is always here."

"One would appreciate a few moments' conversation with him."

"That is impossible."

"My friend and I have come a long way to see him. We have a message from a mutual friend."

"No."

A tall half-caste with a broken nose elbowed Solo aside. "Here, Gaston," he growled. "Attend to your business; there's clients waiting. Three marcs and a large glass of red – and make it quick. We're thirsty."

"If, perhaps, one could allow monsieur the proprietor to decide for himself," Solo began when the barman had filled the order.

"Look – I told you no. Nobody sees the boss without an appointment." He moved away to the espresso machine and began preparing three cups of coffee.

"There would be a certain amount of money involved – for all concerned," Solo called, mastering his temper.

"Keep your money. Tourists are not welcome here, especially American tourists."

"We are not tourists. And I am not American," Illya said suddenly, adding something in an arabic dialect with which Solo was not familiar, although he knew something of the language. He caught something about "the Indian journalist, Anand."

The barman leaned his hands on the counter and thrust his face towards them. "How many times do I have to tell you," he snarled, "that the answer is no? No, no, and again no. Now drink your drinks and shut up, or else get out of – "

He broke off as a high-pitched buzz from below the bar cut through the noise. Reaching down, he unhooked a house phone and held it to his ear. "Yes," he said. "That's right.

Two.... What, right away?... You're quite sure?... As you like, then."

He slammed the instrument back on its hook and scowled at them. "He'll see you," he said curtly, jerking his head towards a bead curtain behind the bar. "This way."

Draining their drinks, the two agents followed him through the curtain and along a dark passageway. They skirted a patio bordered by a grimy glass canopy which rattled under the assault of the rain, pushed through another bead curtain, and found themselves in a softly lit anteroom.

The contrast with the coffee shop was extreme. Subtly coloured Persian rugs strewed the mosaic floor, and the room was dotted with low divans in the oriental style. They could see only one other door: a sheet of beaten copper gleaming dully in a vaulted stone arch. As they entered, a slim man in a waisted suit rose quickly to his feet, one hand hovering near the top button of his jacket. Beneath the tarboosh, his sallow, moustached face was watchful.

"For some reason he's agreed to see these *types*, Ali," the barman said surlily. "You take over from here, eh?"

The slim man nodded, gesturing towards the copper door. As the barman turned and went back through the curtain, he pressed some button concealed in the stonework and the door swung slowly open. Another corridor stretched ahead of them, stone-flagged and illuminated by wrought-iron lamps on brackets.

"After you," the slim man said evenly. Professionally, he kept some distance behind them as they walked past a number of closed doors. Apart from their own footsteps on the stone floor, not a sound disturbed the silence. When they had passed five, Ali called softly: "The next door on the left. Knock four times."

Illya rapped on the teak panels. There was a subdued buzz, terminating in a click – and again the door swung open.

Habib Tufik was a surprise. To begin with, the man was enormous, one of the biggest men Solo had ever seen. He must have weighed well over twenty-stone, the great swell of his belly thrusting against a crumpled sharkskin suit, the fat shoulders merging into a bulging neck. A few strands of red hair were combed across his freckled scalp – and a pair of unexpectedly humorous blue eyes twinkled in among the rolls of pale flesh which formed his face.

The second surprise was that he was sitting in a wheel chair; the third one – that he greeted them in the broadest of County Cork accents.

"Well now, boys," he called cheerfully, "and what can I be doing for you? Come in, come in, and sit you down – if you can find a place, that is. For it's queer and cluttered it's getting to be in here at all!"

He waved a fat hand around the windowless room. It was indeed difficult to find a seat. For the whole area, which was about thirty feet square, seemed at first to be swamped by a great tide of paper. There were a few piles of reference books, matched by corresponding spaces in the bookshelves which filled one entire wall; but most of the litter comprised an apparently endless variety of newspapers, magazines and journals from all over the world – strewing the vast table, overflowing on to chairs and divans, and dotting the floor in untidy heaps.

Most of these, Solo saw, contained marked passages panelled off in pencil, with underlinings and annotations in various colours. Among the piles were dozens of sheets of writing paper covered with scribbled notes, sheaves of clippings, and rolls of teleprinter paper bearing agency messages from Reuter, Havas, Associated Press of America and Tass, the Russian newsagency.

Steel filing cabinets along one wall flanked a modernistic console which looked like the control panel of a recording studio. The remaining two walls – one containing the door through which they had entered, the other pierced by an archway masked by the inevitable bead curtain – were hung with oriental rugs.

The room was airless and hot. The two agents stripped off their soaking raincoats and dropped them by a pile of month-old *Herald Tribunes*. Illya perched on the corner of an ottoman covered in purple silk, and Solo removed copies of *Paris-Match*, *Stern*, *Oggia* and *Izvestia* from a low armchair and sank into it with a sigh of relief.

"'Tis a foul night out there, they tell me," the fat man continued, "and you'll be after needing a spot of refreshment." He clapped his hands three times and then turned to the man in the tarboosh. "That's alright, Ali, thank you," he said. "I'll let you know when these gentlemen are leaving."

The thin man bowed and withdrew, closing the heavy door after him. A moment later, with a rattle of beads, a veiled arab girl of about thirteen with enormous black eyes pushed through the curtain. She was carrying a large brass tray containing tiny cups and saucers, a copper pan full of fragrant coffee, a stone flask, glasses, and a squat bottle half full of pale yellow liquor.

Habib Tufik said something to her in arabic as she cleared a space on the table and set down the tray. He slapped her familiarly on her silken bottom as she giggled and ran off through the curtain.

"Delightful creature!" he said reflectively, staring at the strings of swaying beads. "I keep half a dozen of them to look after me, you know. When you're a big fellow like me, there's nothing more relaxing – nothing at all – than to have three or four – er – But, sure, I'm forgetting me manners! Turkish coffee, now? With a drop of rosewater to settle the grounds? And you'll take a spot of the hard stuff? It's Izzara, the finest liqueur. . . . I have the sweet tooth, as you see!"

Pouring the drinks, he spun the wheel chair with dexterity and propelled himself rapidly to each of them in turn. The eggshell-shaped glasses, Solo saw as he sipped the aromatic liqueur, were held in a fine filigree cage, black with the patina of age.

"You have a most – unusual – establishment here, Monsieur Tufik," he said.

"Sure, and I suppose I have and all. Though if it's the girls you mean . . ."

"I didn't only mean the girls. There's something of a contrast, you'll admit, between the – er – coffee shop and this room. And then there's the electrically controlled doors, the professional gunman outside, the fact that you knew we were here and invited us in just as your barman was about to turn us away . . ."

"Ah, you have to keep a finger on the pulse, boy, in my business – and you have to take precautions, too, you know."

"And just what *is* your business, Monsieur Tufik?" Illya asked.

"Well now, that'd be a question I should rightly ask you. *You're* the ones who asked to see *me*. What d'you want?" The blue eyes were suddenly shrewd and calculating.

Solo decided on the direct approach. "We were given to understand by a friend – a late friend – that you might be able to provide us with some information," he said. "His name was Devananda Anand."

The fat man chuckled in delight, the rolls of flesh around his neck wobbling uncontrollably as he sucked coffee, through pursed lips. "Sure there's a splendid coincidence," he said. "You've come to the right man, then – for information *is* my business! I'm a merchant of information, to be sure: wholesale or retail, in gross or single items. You name it – I'll get it! . . . And let's be quite clear on one point: I'm precisely that; a seller of information. I play no favourites, I take no sides, I offer no loyalty, no allegiances. If a man comes to me and pays for information, I give to him. I don't care who he is. The customer is always right, gentlemen – and my customers come from all over. Police, private detectives, lawyers, intelligence men from here to hell-and-gone – they all come to Habib Tufik."

"That's a fine old Irish name," Solo commented.

"And it's my own, I'll have you know, boy. Me mother was Irish, God rest her poor soul, and indeed I was brought up in Ireland. But me father was a Casablanca man, born and bred – though you'd not think it to look at me, now, would ye?"

"I would not. But I understand you've been here a great number of years, just the same."

"I have and all. The kind of set-up I have here doesn't grow in a day, you know. It's taken a long time to build up. You wouldn't believe how many hundred dollars a week it costs me in wire services and papers alone. . . ." He gestured at the mass of periodicals around the room. ". . . And then of course there's the informers, the hotel porters, the airport people, the travel agency men, and I don't know what-all."

"I would imagine you have a formidable knowledge of

current events all over the world just from reading these," Illya said with a smile.

"Well, you know how it is: you never know when it'll come in useful knowing who's knocking around with whom. The gossip columns – when you add two and two together from different ends of the world – can tell a man a great deal. Then, of course, there's the diplomatic and the political pieces. There's much to read between the lines there."

"And the coffee shop?"

"Perhaps that's the most useful of all. You know the way they used to say, in the big houses like, that if you wanted to know what went on, then you'd ask in the servants' hall? Well, my coffee shop's a bit like the old servants' hall. We get seamen there from the boats, waiters from the embassies, layabouts, porters. All kinds.... Sure, I'm like a recording machine in here, preserving everything that comes in – and the coffee shop's one of my main microphones, as it were."

"As I said before," Solo remarked: "we were impressed with the way you knew about our enquiry."

"And isn't that the simplest thing, though? Wait'll I show you." Tufik wheeled himself across to the console and flicked a switch. A pilot light glowed red on a wide indicator board. "What'll you have?" he asked. "The bar? Second table from the left? The far end where the tough boys stand?"

He thumbed a series of buttons which were ranged across the board. As each one was depressed a coloured light glowed above it and a snatch of conversation boomed from a hi-fi speaker to one side of the console.

"*... asked H.E.'s daughter to slip the package into the diplomatic bag, but the bitch wouldn't play ...*"

"*... Gaston! Three flats and a glass of white! ...*"

"*... and all you have to do, my friend, is listen a bit ...*"

"*... wipe that smile off your face, if I were you, or there's one or two of us'll bloody-well wipe it off for you ...*"

"*... they're flics, that's what they are. Mark my words, that pair are up to no good ...*"

Solo recognized in the last voice the bad-tempered half-caste who had shouldered him aside at the bar. He had noticed the man glaring at Illya and himself before they were brought through, and he had no doubt that they were still the subject of conversation. "Very ingenious," he said. "You have every table wired for sound, and other mikes concealed at strategic points around the room. How do you know when to listen to what?"

Tufik was delighted. He giggled like a schoolboy. "It's good, isn't it?" he crowed. "As to listening, the whole lot are recorded automatically. I have two secretaries who each morning go through the tapes and draw my attention to any interesting stuff." He pointed to two enormous spools revolving at sixteen and two-thirds rpm on a complex tape deck beyond the speaker. "It's multi-track, recording both sides."

"And this, I take it, is information for which you do not pay?"

Tufik burst out laughing. "That's it," he wheezed. "Gratis. That's what it is. This stuff's the bunce to offset all the money I lay out in other directions!"

"I imagine there's one class of information you don't sell."

"Something I can't provide? You name it." The fat man bristled. His professional pride was impugned.

"I mean information about one client's demands – to another."

"Ah, no! 'Twouldn't be right, now, would it? No I couldn't do that at all."

Somewhere, a telephone was ringing. Tufik eventually tracked it down under a heap of colour supplements on the table. "Hallo, hallo . . . It is that . . . Yes, Colonel. And you too . . ." He listened for a few moments and then said crisply: "Yes, I think I can. Just hold on, will you? . . . Now wait . . . where did I put that cutting?"

He hunted among the various piles of papers, wheeling himself around the room with extraordinary speed. At last, with a cry of triumph, he came up with a clipping in what looked like Japanese characters. "Got it!" he announced proudly into the mouthpiece. "A model girl from Tokyo who works a lot in New York. Name's Umino Takimoto. They stayed at the Imperial in . . . let's see . . . yes, from the 21st to the 28th of March, last year . . ."

"Military attaché," he said as he put the instrument down. "Now there's some poor fellow's going to have the bite put on him!"

"Your work must make you somewhat . . . unpopular . . . in certain quarters," Illya commented.

"It does that. There's plenty would try and stop me, believe you me, boy. . . . They nearly did once: that's why you see me here in this contraption. 'Twas when I was younger and stronger, and I had a mind to put a stop to a gang of boyos was spreading lying tales about me behind me back, see. They was tryin' to put me out of business and I went up to sort them out – only they had more friends than I did and somebody put the boot in. . . . Result: a spinal injury and partial paralysis."

"You seem to have plenty of protection now, though."

"Ah, sure. I never go out now. I have my girls and my work – I keep in touch, as you might say! Then there's Ali and Gaston and a couple more good ones to look after me. Wait'll I show you. . . . "

He clapped his hands twice and called, "*Charles!*"

Behind a blank space in the bookshelves a shutter slid open and the muzzle of a machine pistol poked into the room, capped by the long snout of a silencer. Above it, watchful eyes glinted in the reflected light.

"All right, Charles, thank you: just a demonstration," Tufik said over his shoulder. The shutter snapped shut again. "But there you are, you see. My visitors are covered all the while they're here. . . . Still, I don't want to rush you gentlemen – but I have callers expected. What did you want to know?"

"I gather you must have helped Devananda Anand," Solo said easily. "Perhaps he was a client?"

"These many years. You'd not have got in, mind, if I hadn't heard you mention his name out there. This is strictly a personal recommendation business. I don't know who he was working for – that's not my affair. But I helped him many times."

"He was – shall we say? – a colleague," Solo said tightly. "I am following up his leads, as he hasn't been replaced in this station yet. My question is simple: Anand was trailing a consignment of a certain commodity that I have reason to believe left here on a camel train for Alexandria yesterday or today. I want to know the name and address of a contact in Alex who can put me in touch with someone who'll be able to finger the caravan for me when it gets there. And, for good measure, I'd like confirmation of what the consignment is and the fact that it *is* on that caravan. Can you oblige?"

"I can. Now we have two systems in this business: we have the subscription account – which is fine for clients like that military attaché who constantly wants snippets of information. But it'll hardly interest you.... Then we have the flat fee."

"Which is?"

"For every isolated piece of important information, irrespective of how simple or complicated, one thousand dollars. It may seem a lot – but, as you see, I have my overheads."

Solo took a wallet from his breast pocket and counted out ten hundred dollar bills. He laid them on the table.

"... plus twenty-five per cent service charge," Tufik continued suavely. "One of the reasons I got such good protection is that the boys there are on a percentage. That's why Gaston spurned your little bribe!"

The agent opened the wallet again and took out two more hundreds and five tens, placing them on top of the bills already on the table.

"... and one per cent state tax."

"You're not serious!"

"Certainly I am. There's different kinds of protection, boy."

Solo shook his head in disbelief as he pulled two crumpled five dollar bills from his pocket.

"Right." Habib Tufik's voice was suddenly brisk. "I can answer your questions, as it happens, without any research. The consignment – let's just say it's highly radioactive – did leave today, at dawn. It's in a lead canister that's much heavier than it looks."

"Good. And the contact?"

"You'll be travelling by air?... Fine. Now, the day after tomorrow, take the Corniche and you'll find Stanley Bay –

it's the usual sort of bathing beach with a sea-front and a parapet and I don't know what-all. At the far end, on the landward side of the road, there's a tatty little restaurant called La Terraza. It stands all by itself; you couldn't miss it. Order a Turkish coffee and an Izarra and wait there. You'll be joined by a little man called Mahmoud, who works in the Weights and Measures office. I think he'll be able to help you."

"What time the day after tomorrow? I can't drink Izarra all day."

"Well now, the harbour at Alexandria's a very interesting place, they do say. If you was to take a walk down there in the morning, say at about eleven thirty, I shouldn't be surprised if someone managed to get a message to you about that."

Solo rose to his feet. "Thank you very much," he said.

"A pleasure, sir. There's a thing *you* might be able to tell me now, before you go: talking to your friend, who met with such a sad end, I found he referred several times to an organization which calls itself THRUSH. Now I never heard tell of that. Do you know what it is?"

"You won't have heard of it because it never appears in newspapers or on agency tapes," Solo said with a wintry smile. "But it's a tremendously powerful organization just the same."

"You don't say! And just exactly what is it?"

"It's . . . How on earth would you define THRUSH, Illya?"

"It is a supra-nation," Kuryakin said. "A syndicate of scientists, industrialists, mathematicians, political theorists and would-be dictators, all of them brilliant brains with respectable cover occupations; but all of them dedicated to what those who moralize would call evil."

"And where are they based?"

"Everywhere." Illya got up and crossed the room to a large globe standing on a side table. He spun the sphere and jabbed a finger towards the revolving surface. "Anywhere I care to stop that globe, my finger will be pointing at a territory containing a THRUSH satrap."

"In the name of God, what's that?"

"An undercover cell – it may be a manufacturing complex,

a university, a chain of stores, anything. It'll carry out the purpose for which it was ostensibly set up. But underneath, it will have a secret life of its own: to further the aims of THRUSH."

"And what would they be, for God's sake?"

"Quite simply, to dominate the earth.... They work for no-one; they have no allies – only enemies. So far as THRUSH is concerned, either you're one of them, or you're to be ruled or destroyed. Which is not to say they won't help the East against the West, or vice versa, if it serves their purpose."

"They have an enormous treasury," Solo put in, "financed by a vast series of enterprises, legal and criminal. And they can command the latest in weapons and communications – whole armies if need be, if the Council considered they could be useful."

"The Council?"

"The ruling body; the super-brains at the top."

"And could you be telling me, now, the names of one or two members of this Council? – a couple of them normally based in this part of the world, for instance?"

"Certainly. The information will cost you one thousand dollars. There is no service charge."

Habib Tufik grinned suddenly. "Good night, gentlemen," he said. "It's been a pleasure seeing you. A real pleasure."

He sat for some minutes after they had gone, staring pensively at the papers scattered on his table. At last he reached slowly for the telephone. "Hallo?" he said. "Get me the Commissariat of Police, will you?"

CHAPTER FIVE

CONTACT WITH THE ENEMY

THE first attack came – rather as Solo had anticipated – almost as soon as they left Habib Tufik's premises. Broken-nose and his cronies were conspicuous by their absence as they threaded their way out through the din in the coffee shop. He caught Illya by the arm as they pushed open the wrought-iron gate leading to the court. "Keep your eyes open," he said warningly. "I have a hunch . . . "

"The half-caste we heard on the speaker?"

Solo nodded. "I don't know, mind you. I just have a feeling."

"Surely you don't think THRUSH are on to us already, Napoleon?"

"I don't know. Could be. Or it could be just that the fellow doesn't like our type and really thinks we are police spies. Or again, he might think we have money. You're always in danger of getting rolled at night in this part of the town. They looked a pretty villainous bunch to me."

"If it *was* THRUSH, would you suspect our fat friend?"

"Of giving us away? No, I don't think so. I don't think his ignorance of THRUSH was faked – and, anyway, I should imagine he plays a fair game by his own odd standards. He'd be out of business otherwise."

" 'Faithful to thee, Cynara, in my fashion'," Illya quoted softly.

"You and your night-school . . . " Solo began chidingly – when suddenly the fight began without an instant's warning.

They had anticipated an ambush somewhere in the dark, cobbled alley leading downhill to the place where they had left the taxi. In fact, the attack came from above. . . . Half a dozen men leaped down upon them from a balcony over the archway which connected the alley and the court, and in a moment all was confusion.

Solo was sent sprawling to the wet cobbles by a violent

blow in the back. He rolled with the fall, drawing his knees up to protect his stomach, so that the follow-up man jumping for his belly tripped and fell heavily beside him. The agent chopped him viciously, flat-handed, to the throat and twisted eel-like to his feet as two more men rushed him with upraised arms.

Kuryakin was on the far side of the alley. His assailant had misjudged his leap and the Russian had been sent spinning across the narrow thoroughfare, to slam against the wall, where he was now desperately trying to fend off three attackers bent on clawing him down.

Solo dragged his gun – the semi-automatic Special which fired bullets either singly or in bursts – from its shoulder holster. But before he could thumb off the safety catch, a paralysing knock on the right arm dropped it from his nerveless fingers. Blows were raining down on his head and shoulders and from the corner of his eye he saw the lamplight gleaming on the length of lead pipe which had crippled his arm.

He drove his left elbow into his assailant's solar plexus, brought his knee up to parry a kick for his groin, and chopped down again on the man, who had fallen but was now groping for Solo's gun on the cobbles. He grunted and collapsed on his face as Solo kicked the weapon spinning into the middle of the alley.

With a heave of his shoulders, the agent broke momentarily free and piled a left with all his weight behind it, straight to the jaw of the man with the lead pipe. The attacker dropped like a stone, his cosh clattering to the ground.

Illya had butted one man in the face – he sat in the roadway with blood from a smashed nose streaming through his fingers – and was now trading punches with the remaining pair as Solo was left facing the half-caste, who now carried a knife with a wickedly curved blade.

The agent backed warily away along the wall, his eyes fixed on the murderous face. With a tigerish bound, the half-caste was on him. Solo twisted aside as the knife blade scraped sparks from the wall, The assassin whirled and crouched for another spring, knife arm held wide. Sidling farther along the wall, Solo found himself in front of a recessed doorway. As his antagonist attacked again, keeping one hand on each doorpost Solo backed momentarily into the entry and then – using his hands as levers – launched himself feet first, like a wrestler, at the half-caste.

Steel ripped through his jacket as his heels caught the man full in the chest, knocking him to the ground. It was no time for Queensberry Rules. The agent scrambled upright, stamped on the man's knife hand and took a running fly-kick at his head. The metal-capped tip of his shoe connected just below the ear – and broken-nose was out for the count.

As Solo turned towards Illya, he saw the Russian suddenly go limp and collapse to the ground. He increased his pace – but Kuryakin had been feinting. He rolled out from under the legs of the two men who had been pinning him to the wall, and was on his feet two yards behind them before they realized they had been tricked. As they turned, his hand dipped into his pocket and reappeared holding what looked like a pistol-grip cigarette lighter. There were two soft, flat explosions. The thugs halted, staggered, and subsided to the ground at his feet.

"Too bad they were only sleep darts," Solo panted. "Come on, let's get out of here – Oh! Wait a minute. My gun . . ."

As they searched the dark alleyway, they realized for the first time since they had left the coffee shop that it was no longer raining. Throughout the fight, which had lasted perhaps two and a half minutes, not a light had come on, not a window had been opened, not an enquiring head had appeared. Now they were suddenly aware of the persistent trickling and splashing and dripping of water from eaves and broken guttering all around them. From somewhere over the rooftops, a motor horn blared momentarily.

But Solo's gun was nowhere to be found.

"I kicked it hard," Solo said. "It may have spun further than I thought. I wonder . . ."

"Perhaps one of the – er – casualties is lying on it, Napoleon. Shall I turn them over to have a look?" Illya suggested.

Solo glanced back at the scene of combat. Broken-nose and the two sleep-dart victims lay where they had fallen. The man with the smashed face still sat sobbing into his bloodstained hands. But the other two men Solo had felled were stirring and groaning.

"No," he said decidedly. "Forget it. For all we know, there may be reinforcements on the way. Let sleeping dogs lie – in every sense of the term. We'll be on our way while we can."

Half running, half walking, they limped down the hill. Illya's face was bruised and swollen and there was a jagged cut on his forehead. His collar was torn open and one sleeve had been ripped from his raincoat. Solo was less obviously marked, but there was an ugly contusion at one side of his head, his body ached all over and his right arm was still useless. The half-caste's knife had slashed clean through waterproof and jacket, and the chamois holster for the missing gun – which had probably saved his life – was sliced in two. Both of them were covered in mud and filth from head to foot.

As they rounded the corner in the street, they halted abruptly. By the light from the intersection where their taxi had turned they could see three men in wide-brimmed hats and long raincoats advancing up the hill towards them.

Before they had time to think, there came the plop of a silenced revolver and a bullet struck the cobbles by Illya's feet, screeching into the night.

"Quick!" Solo gasped. "Back round the corner!"

They scrambled round the bend into temporary shelter – to hear, farther up the hill, a hoarse shout. The two thugs Solo had knocked down were on their feet. Faint lamplight gleamed for a second on steel.

"Caught in the middle, by God," Solo exclaimed. He looked desperately around him at the blank-walled alley. "Up there! Quickly!"

He leaped for a low wrought-iron balcony projecting above a barred doorway and grasped the sill with his fingers. For a moment his numb right arm gave way and he hung by one hand. Then he managed to swing one leg up and replace the wrist of his damaged arm between the bars. From there, painfully, he levered himself to a position in which he could haul himself over the railings. A moment later Kuryakin dropped to the floor of the balcony beside him.

Light seeped through the slats of the flimsy shutters across the french windows. Illya dropped on to one knee and peered through. "It's all right," he whispered; "the glass doors behind are wide open."

Solo nodded. Footsteps clattered on the cobbles as voices called out in the dark alleyway below. He drew back his right foot and slammed his heel through the flimsy crosspieces which were about half-way up the shutters. The wood splintered and gave inwards. Illya thrust his arm through the jagged space and twisted the catch, jerking the door open towards him.

Inside the squalid bedroom behind the shutters, a fat woman with hennaed hair had been admiring herself in a flyblown pier-glass. She jumped to her feet, flabby body quivering, as the two agents tumbled through the aperture. The face painted over her features cracked open in a smile.

"Not without an appointment, messieurs, *if* you please," she croaked with mock severity.

"Not to worry, darling: we're just passing through." Solo grinned over his shoulder as they made for the door.

"Mind, I could make an exception ... " the woman began.

But Solo and Illya were already half-way down the dingy passageway outside. Doors sealed it off along each side and at either end.

"There must be a way to the stairs somewhere," Solo muttered. "Come on – we'll try the end one."

From somewhere on the floor below a persistent hammering began. Nearer, there was a faint echo of music.

They flung open the door at the end of the corridor. It led to another bedroom. A couple were in bed listening to a transistor radio. In the far corner, a baby slept in a cot.

The man started up in terror, clutching the bedclothes across his chest. "I don't want no trouble, man," he stammered. "I don't want to get involved in no – "

"The stairs," Solo rapped, interrupting him. "Where are the stairs?"

"Look, I don't want no trouble. I don't want to get involved."

"The *stairs*?"

"If you want money, man, I ain't got none. If you're from the police, this here's my wife and that's our kid. I don't want no – "

"*In the name of God, where are the stairs?*"

Suddenly realizing what a frightening sight they must be, Illya turned to the girl. "Look," he said gently, "there's a gang of men after us who want to murder us. All we want to know is – which door leads to the staircase?"

The girl stared at them through sleepy eyes. "Second on the right," she murmured. "Turn left at the bottom for the back entrance."

"Thanks. Sorry for the interruption."

"Be my guest," the girl said laconically. "Edward, for God's sake lie down."

As they yanked open the door leading to the stairs, they saw the fat woman watching them from the doorway of her room, her hands on her hips.

The hammering on the front door had stopped. Bullets splintered through the woodwork as they charged down the stone steps, turned left, and pelted along another passage. The rear entrance was an archway leading off a crude kitchen where an old arab woman slept upright in a chair by the stove.

They crossed a small yard, climbed on to a wall, using the refuse bins to stand on, and dropped ten feet to a sunken alley on the far side. The passage traced an irregular course between tall buildings for several hundred yards, finally terminating in a flight of steps leading down to a brightly lit street. Half an hour later, they were sneaking up the back stairs of their hotel. . . .

The second attack came the following morning. Solo had coded a message to cable to Waverly and they were on their way to the main post office in a taxi. Banks of high cloud scudded across a sunny sky, though the drying road was still greasy from the previous night's rain.

They were only a few blocks from their destination when a Renault 16 passed them, its loading window at the back propped open. It was Illya who noticed the car slacken speed momentarily when it was about fifty yards ahead. Two men were manoeuvering something by the open window. Then, as the Renault accelerated viciously away, a square, black, heavy object fell to the road and came spinning in their path.

There was no time for speech. Kuryakin's hand darted forward over the back of the driver's seat. Grasping the handbrake, he hauled on it with all his strength.

With its rear wheels suddenly locked, with a screaming of tyres the heavy cab slewed sideways across the slippery road. The back end broke away, the startled driver over-corrected, and the taxi – with Illya still wrenching white-faced at the lever – turned completely round. It shot backwards into a traffic island, where it slammed into a bollard and turned slowly over on to its side.

The noise of the crash was drowned in the explosion, which blew a ten-foot crater in the roadway. Miraculously, nobody was hurt.

"That settles it, then," Solo said soon afterwards, as he picked granules of toughened glass from his hair. "We'll forget the cable; we'll forget the direct flight we booked. If we go straight back to the hotel to pick up our luggage, we can just make the earlier Royal Air Maroc Caravelle to Rome – and we can change planes there and fly to Cairo...."

By midnight, a hired car had deposited them in Alexandria.

CHAPTER SIX

EXIT MR MAHMOUD

THE sea at Stanley Bay was oyster-coloured and smooth. Every few minutes it gathered enough strength to flop listlessly into a miniscule wave, which sank into the sand before it could recede. Half a mile offshore, water and sky merged, horizonless, into a uniform sheet of grey.

Moisture beaded the cane tables and chairs of the Terraza, filming the shiny walls and misting the urns behind the counter. Apart from a couple of students necking at the back of the cafe, Solo and Kuryakin were the only customers. Dutifully, they ordered Turkish coffee and Izarra, gazing through steamy windows towards the beach. On the deserted terrace outside, a United Arab Republic flag drooped from a peeling flagstaff.

They had spent the morning on the waterfront, strolling erratically along the moss-covered wharves and gazing at the long lines of big ships ranked in the huge dock, sometimes pausing to stare at a forest of masts and cordage outside the Yacht Club in the inner basin. Seawards, a fleet of fishing boats with liver-coloured sails cleared the corridor between the moored ships and headed for open water. Once a sentry had warned them sternly away from a bay where two UAR gunboats were refuelling. Otherwise nobody had come near them.

It had been almost midday when a stone wrapped in paper, thrown from somewhere behind them, had landed on the cobbles at their feet. They swung round. Above the hammering activity of the port, flocks of pigeons wheeled between palms and the onion-shaped minarets of the city; but nobody was in sight.

Solo unwrapped the paper. There were no words on it – just a meticulously drawn clock face with the hands pointing to 3.45.

And now it was a quarter past four and they were on their third order of coffee and liqueurs. Illya smacked his lips and grimaced. "Very pleasant," he said dubiously, "once. But a small amount, as the English say, travels a great distance."

"A little goes a long way," Solo corrected automatically. "I hope this man Mahmoud is coming. It'd be a devil of a job picking up a cold trail from here!" For the twentieth time, he stared out of the window at the livid sea.

Then came a rustling of tyres on gravel. A moment later, a thin man in a cream alpaca suit carried a bicycle on to the terrace and propped it against a railing. Pushing through the bead curtain, he glanced quickly around the sleazy room. He was a ferrety little man with glasses and a ragged moustache smudged across his pale face. The students were still immersed in each other. A table full of middle-aged tourists who had come in shortly before chattered together in French. For a second, the shifty eyes rested on the agents' table: the yellow fluid in the small glasses, the copper pan of coffee. Then he walked quickly across and sat down in a vacant chair.

"Mr Mahmoud?" Solo queried politely.

"No names, please," the little man said hurriedly, glancing over his shoulder. "My apologies for the delay. As you see, things are happening." He dragged a folded newspaper from an inner pocket and spread it on the table.

It was that day's copy of *Al Ahram*, folded back to an inner page. Below the fold, an item had been ringed in red marker. "BOMB OUTRAGES IN CASABLANCA," Solo read. "*Following an unexplained explosion in a main street of the city yesterday morning, Casablanca police were today trying to piece together the reasons for a bomb blast which destroyed a coffee shop in the old part of the town during the early hours of this morning. Among the wreckage, which extended to a building behind the premises, were discovered the bodies of six young girls and three men . . .* "

Solo stopped reading and dropped the paper back on the table. "So someone got him at last," he sighed. "I see what you mean."

Mahmoud's fingers were trembling. "Not someone," he said. "*They* got him. . . . He – he told me what it was you wanted. I can give you a name – but it will cost you plenty."

"I expected that."

"I've got a wife and family, and I want to get out. When I agreed at first, I never expected . . . It'll cost you plenty," the little man repeated, mopping his brow with a large silk handkerchief.

"Okay, so it'll cost me plenty. So can you deliver, that's the point?"

"Yes, but I'm not entirely sure what you want to do. This bomb thing, you see, has altered things. They must know somebody's on the trail. In fact, I know they do, because they've switched plans. . . . I have friends in the police and Movement Control . . . that's why I was so late. I was checking – "

"Sure, sure, sure. Just tell me what you found out."

"They've taken the – consignment – in which you're interested away from the caravan. They landed a helicopter and took it away."

"They must be rattled to do something so obvious. D'you know where the helicopter went?"

"To Khartoum, in the Sudan. What do you want to do? How can I help you?"

"What happens to the stuff in Khartoum?"

"I don't know. I think . . . I believe it will be concealed on another caravan which leaves there in a few days."

"What caravan? Heading where? How can I contact it?"

"I don't know. I don't know where it's going. But I can give you a name in Khartoum. What do you want to do?"

"I speak some arabic," Solo said slowly. "I want the name of someone who can identify that caravan; someone who can get me to the place it starts from, fix me up with the right kind of disguise, papers and so on, and finally fix it so that I can take someone's place on the journey: bribe someone to change places with me, maybe."

Mahmoud thought for a moment, drumming his fingers on the table. "There's an Englishman called Rodney Marshel," he said at last. "He lives in Khartoum – local correspondent for Eros newsagency, I think. He could help. I'm not sure about the papers, though. What kind did you want?"

"Two lots. One to justify my presence on the caravan . . . "

"Oh, arab papers. Marshel could handle that alright."

"... and another set which would keep me right with the authorities if I had to leave the caravan and reassume some – er – Western identity."

"Ah. That's more difficult. The Sudan's a troubled area just now, particularly in the south, and strangers are unwelcome."

"Exactly. That's why I need the best papers."

"Marshel couldn't help you there. You'll have to go to someone more important . . . a man called Hassan Hamid – *very* important; he has a high post. He also has a high standard of living. He is very interesting in money."

"As if I didn't know," Solo murmured.

"Hamid can give you any papers you want – at a price. But you'll have to have a good cover reason. And don't on any account mention the caravan side of the business, because he's the – "

Mahmoud was abruptly hurled backwards from his chair, to crash against the wall. He slid to the floor, blood blooming like an exotic flower from the lapel of his pale suit. In the same moment, their shocked senses registered the crack of a distant shot. Shards of glass tinkled to the floor from the shattered window.

Illya was out on the terrace by the time Solo had reached Mahmoud's body. A moment later, he was back, shaking his head.

From across the bay, the sound of a tuned engine accelerating fiercely in bottom gear cut through the murmurs of horrified astonishment from the other customers in the cafe now surrounding Solo and the body.

"Somebody in an Alfa-Romeo," Kiryakin said. "They were using a rifle with a telescopic sight."

There was blood on Solo's hands. "But, my God," he exclaimed, looking up at the Russian, "the muzzle velocity of that gun . . . ! To send a man crashing back all that way . . ."

Illya nodded. "I know," he said. "It was probably a Mannlicher. He's quite dead, of course?"

"Beyond all recall." Solo rose to his feet and looked down at the sprawled figure. "Poor devil. Rough on his wife and kids, too. He was so scared, he didn't even ask for his money." He hesitated, and then drew a sealed envelope from his breast pocket and tucked it inside the dead man's jacket. "I guess there are enough witnesses here to stop anyone from lifting it," he said.

While Solo and Illya were identifying themselves privately to the police, the two students left the cafe. Half a mile away, they went into another cafe and the girl walked through to a telephone booth. She dialled a number and waited. Then, "You were a little late," she said. "He had already begun to talk.... But I don't think he had time to say much."

On the plane to Khartoum that evening, Solo turned to Illya and said, "You realize what was the most extraordinary piece of information given to us by Mahmoud?"

"You mean about Marshel?"

"Yes," Solo said soberly. "An Englishman called Rodney Marshel – *our* man in the Sudan..."

CHAPTER SEVEN

MARSHEL AID

"What I want to know, Marshel," Napoleon Solo said crisply, "is exactly why your name should have been given to me by an Alexandria informer? Why should you have been the first person he thought of when I asked him for a contact to help me in certain illegal activities? How come you are supposed to be the man who knows all about the movements of contraband camel trains? And if you do, why in God's name haven't you reported it to Waverly? What kind of game are you playing, anyway?"

"Well, I mean, because I wasn't asked to, actually," Rodney Marshel said, flushing slightly. He was a tall, thin young man with a lock of pale hair falling forward over one eye.

"Weren't asked to? Well, for God's sake! What are you supposed to be doing here for us, then, if it's not to report things like that?"

"My briefing is to report anything I think would be of interest, Mr Solo. It didn't occur to me that this would be, that's all."

"But, good grief..."

"By and large that means a situation report every month," Marshel continued reasonably. "Plus fuller stuff on anything specific that I'm asked to cover. Plus liaison with people like yourself and Mr Kuryakin when it's required. After all, I'm not an Enforcement Agent like you."

"I know, I know. But surely shipments of Uranium 235..."

"I didn't know it was 235 – only that it was some radioactive substance," the young man said sullenly. "I'm sorry."

"I know you're only part-time for the Command," Solo said, "but even so – admitting that New York was at fault in not letting you know – even so, I should have thought..." He broke off with an exasperated shrug.

"You said yourself, actually, that you'd no idea until

yesterday the stuff would be coming to Khartoum – when Mahmoud told you."

"That's true. It doesn't get away from the fact that you should have reported it on your own initiative."

"Look, Mr Solo: I can't report everything shady that happens in Khartoum," Marshel argued. "That would choke the airwaves every day. I mean, so I made an error of judgement, that's all."

"I suppose so."

Solo rose to his feet and walked to the french windows of the hotel room. Beyond the dense shade cast by the balcony awning concrete buildings across the street shimmered in the glaring heat. From six floors below, the rumble of afternoon traffic drifted up.

"So far as Mahmoud knowing my name is concerned," the voice drawled on behind him, "I really can't see what you're worrying about."

"Oh, can't you?"

"Absolutely not. I mean, you know my cover's as a stringer for the Eros newsagency – well, that's a job I actually have to do, you know. I have to file stories every day. Mahmoud's simply one of my informants, that's all – *was* one of my informants, rather."

"Did he know you worked with U.N.C.L.E.?"

"Of course not," Marshel said heatedly. "I'm not a complete idiot, Mr Solo. He was just a common informer: you pay for it, he'll give it to you. Like your man in Casablanca. . . . So far as he was concerned, I needed information for my news stories – and, of course, for other reasons."

"Such as?"

"Well, naturally he must have reasoned that I had other interests – with the sort of questions I sometimes had to ask, he could hardly have avoided it. For all I know, he thought I worked for MI6 or for the West Germans. But, as I say, his kind don't ask questions – they just take the money and go. . . . Obviously, though, since he knew the *kind* of things that interested me, he surmised I might be able to help you."

"This informing business with Mahmoud," Solo said meaningly, eyeing Marshel's immaculately cut sharkskin suit, "it wouldn't have been a two-way traffic, by any chance?"

"I hardly think that question deserves an answer, Mr Solo," the young man said, flipping the hair out of his eye with a jerk of his head and flushing a deeper red.

Solo peeled off his own linen jacket and dropped it on the floor. "Okay," he said, grinning. "Question out of order. Sorry, Marshel – I guess the heat's getting me down. It's a bit of a change from the coast." He loosened his tie and crossed the room to a trolley of drinks. "What'll it be?" he asked. "Another Bacardi and lime?"

"Thank you."

"Right," Solo said when they were settled again, ice clinking in the tall glasses. "While we're waiting for Kuryakin, perhaps you'll tell me what you *can* do for me."

"I fancy we should be able to manage, as a matter of fact," Marshel said, looking Solo up and down judiciously. "You are medium height, you've got fairly deep-set, fairly big brown eyes; you have a . . . decided . . . cast of feature. And best of all your hair is very dark. With the right sort of stain all over, and a fringe of beard to offset that chin, you'll pass, after my boy's had a go at you. How's your arabic?"

"Passable."

"Good. You'd better be a pilgrim, though. They keep to themselves and hardly speak on these jaunts. You might be faulted on accent otherwise."

"A pilgrim! Where to, for Heaven's sake?"

"There's a sect that beetle off to some shrine just north of the Congo border every couple of months. They go with the trade caravans for safety's sake."

"And there's a party of them in *our* caravan?"

"So I believe. In any case, that's the only way you could join without comment."

"How d'you mean?"

"Well, I'm afraid the only way it can be done is to substitute yourself for some joker who's already signed on, as it were. They can't be bribed; they're much too religious. But there's a certain police captain who can be bribed. And the drill is, you get a set of papers to match some chap's who's already on the list . . . and then the police captain runs the chap in on some pretext and keeps him in custody until the caravan's gone. Meanwhile, there you are in his place."

"It seems a trifle rough on the chap," Solo said drily.

"Yes, well, it's a pity; but they let him go after a couple of days anyway. Too expensive to feed them in jail. . . . They're used to incomprehensible police behaviour in this part of the world," Marshel said apologetically. "I'm afraid it's the only way."

"I'd rather do it without putting some innocent man in jail – even for a couple of days."

"Well, leave it to me. I'll see what I can fix."

"Right. And you know someone who can get me to the right place at the right time? – and the right caravan?"

"Oh, yes. It's some way south of the city. We'll get you there. Can you – er – can you ride a camel?"

"If pushed."

"Splendid. I should warn you that, if you're discovered – er – impersonating a pilgrim, the consequences can be deuced unpleasant. These arab johnnies are very strong on religion – the accursed infidel and all that, you know. You'd have to leg it like hell for the bush."

"I'll have to worry about that when it happens."

"Quite. I just thought I'd mention it."

"One other thing: I lost my gun in that fracas at Casablanca – and my holster was carved to ribbons. We have plenty of other little devices, but I'm short of a pistol of some sort. Can you fix me up?"

"I could let you have a Mauser. It's blasted heavy, but it's quite a handy thing. Probably improvise you a holster, too."

"Great. And I'll keep in touch with you by radio. Our little battery transmitters are far too weak to reach home, of course. You'll pass on my messages to Waverly in the normal way."

"Yes, can do."

"Okay," Solo said. "Here's to the great illusion!" He raised his glass.

Three miles away on the other side of the city, in a shuttered villa behind tall hedges of tamarisk, Illya Kuryakin was being ushered into a study furnished in ornate luxury. The man at the glass-topped desk was lean and dark, a hairline moustache emphasizing the chiselled planes of his mouth. Above his head, a huge horizontal fan revolved slowly in the hot, dry air.

"Solo?" he said, glancing at the card Illya had handed in. "That's an unusual name, Monsieur."

"It is an old Russian name," Illya said unblushingly. "From the province of Khirgiztan, originally."

"And the given name which precedes it – especially unusual for one of your nationality, I imagine?" Hassan Hamid said in Russian.

"In memory of my great-great-great grandfather, who commanded one of the units of the Imperial forces instrumental in defeating the French dictator after the burning of Moscow in 1813," Kuryakin said in the same language. "I perceive from your accent that you learned your Russian in Leningrad."

Hamid smiled. "You will forgive me, Monsieur," he said smoothly, returning to French. "In my position one is at times at the mercy of impostors. One likes to be sure of those with whom one deals."

"Naturally."

"I may say that I do not usually receive persons unknown to me personally. However, since you mentioned the name of – shall we say a mutual friend? – of great eminence, and since, to be honest, your own name intrigued me, I made an exception."

"It is an honour to receive such flattering consideration from a highly-placed person," Illya said fulsomely. "And in particular that he should allow himself to be intruded upon at home."

"There are certain ... transactions ... better approached in the informality of the home, Monsieur."

"Precisely."

"Touching upon which, in what way may I assist you, Monsieur Solo?"

"I have a desire to visit the southern part of your agreeable country."

"Indeed? May one ask why?"

"It is said that there are certain mineral deposits," Illya said carefully, "to the south and west of the El Marra massif.

It appears, moreover, that these might be well worth exploitation by those with practically unlimited resources. The lignite veins, for example, are said to be by no means as poor as the reference books would have us believe. The bauxite, too, is of interest to those requiring aluminium – to say nothing of more – er – esoteric ores."

"And you represent such an interest?"

"I do. Those co-operating with my gov – with my principals, would find themselves well rewarded. There is a great deal of money involved. A very great deal."

Hassan Hamid leaned back in his steel and leather chair. His tongue flicked once rapidly around his well-shaped lips. "Your – ah – principals have charged you with the task of verifying these reports?" he asked.

"Yes. I imagine I need not elaborate?"

"No, no, no. Indeed not. But, in this exploratory stage, how can I help you?"

"I understand there is a certain amount of dissidence in the area. I would not wish, during my researches, to run foul either of rebels or of your efficient troops policing the region. Apart from which, in the normal way, I imagine you would scarcely welcome strangers there."

"There are one or two cut-throat bands of renegade blacks," Hassan Hamid said carelessly, flicking a speck of dust from his lapel. "We Muslims in the north are continually being misrepresented by the backward negroes of the south. Agitators are sent in to stir up trouble, and the poor fools fancy themselves exploited. But there is nothing which could be called a rebellion proper. . . . Nevertheless, it is true that a foreigner wandering there could run into trouble."

"Just so. And since it was not considered desirable at this stage to make an official approach at governmental level, I am here to ask your help in the granting of some form of *laissez-passer* which would at once identify me, justify my existence in that area, and assure those whom it might concern that I was under your protection, as it were."

Hassan Hamid rose from behind the desk, moving elegantly across the room to a large wall map flanked by a coat of arms and the Sudanese flag. "I gather the areas in question would be, roughly, here . . . and here . . . and perhaps here?" he said, tapping the map with a manicured finger.

"Yes," Illya said. "Would you care for a Russian cigarette?"

"Thank you, I do not smoke. Please do so yourself, if you feel inclined."

Kuryakin murmured his thanks and placed one of the brown cardboard tubes between his lips. He seemed to have some trouble in manipulating the heavy bronze lighter, for it took several attempts before the spark produced a flame.

Hamid waited politely by the map, tapping his teeth with a gold pencil. "Yes, I think that can be arranged," he said at last when Illya's cigarette was drawing properly. "If you could go tonight to the police station at this address" – he moved back to the desk and scribbled a few lines on a sheet from an ivory-framed memo pad – "the necessary documents will be waiting for you. Please take your passport to identify yourself. The staff will themselves take your photograph and attach a copy to the papers . . . just to ensure the right person gets them, you understand. And you should also present this . . ." He wrote something on a second memo sheet, tore both sheets from the pad, and handed them to Illya.

"You are very kind."

"It is a pleasure. . . . Oh, there is one thing: such extracurricular activities regrettably involve the participant in certain expenses. There are various charges, payable to the departments involved, inseparable from the issue of such papers, I am afraid." He shrugged.

"Not at all. It is to be expected. I have already trespassed too much on your generosity – but, since it is out of office hours and I have no other way of paying them, would it be too much of an imposition if I were to entrust these monies to you for disbursement in the right quarters?"

"In the circumstances," Hamid said suavely, "I would be prepared to waive protocol and perform that service for you."

Illya reached for his wallet.

Later, rejoining Solo in their hotel, he unloaded the spool from the tiny camera which had been concealed in his cigarette lighter and developed the film. Two of the shots he had taken were too blurred to be of use. The other three were as clear as a bell: two profiles of Hamid pointing at the map of Sudan, and one full face of him standing by the flag and tapping his teeth with the gold pencil.

"We'll print them up," Solo said. "Just in case..."

After that, Kuryakin dismantled the miniature lapel microphone and the fine wire lead connecting it with the cigarette-case tape-recorder in his breast pocket, and they played back the recording of his interview. They found that the tape had run out in the middle of Hamid's sentence about "extra-curricular activities" involving the participant in "certain expenses."

"That is exasperating," Illya said. "We've lost the part where he agrees to take the money himself. Also the amount, which came later. There's nothing there we could use as a lever if ever we needed to – it's just a man going out of his way to accommodate a foreigner, on the face of it."

"Never mind," Solo said, clapping him on the shoulder. "What we have is very interesting, as it is. Your Russian act was inspired!"

"Yes, I suppose it could have been worse. Thank goodness for sixteen and two-thirds rpm."

At eight-thirty, Solo took Hamid's scrawled note of introduction, his own passport, and a further supply of money to the address Illya had been given. He was back in less than an hour with an imposing document which called upon all whom it might concern to let Napoleon Solo, photo attached, freely pass without let or hindrance at the peril of enraging His Excellency Hassan Hamid; and so on and so on.

"Funny thing, security," he said to Illya. "They take every precaution under the sun to ensure that the guy who gets the document is the one whose passport they have, and that the mug on the document is the same as the one on the passport – even to the extent of taking the pictures themselves. But there's no check whatever on whether the guy with the passport calling for the thing is the same as the one who originally asked for it!"

"Thank goodness," Illya said soberly.

The next morning Marshel came to tell them that one of his spies had found out that the caravan was headed for Wadi Elmira, where the contingent of pilgrims was to leave the main body and head south.

"There's only one other trail out of Elmira," he said. "Southwest to Halakaz and Gabotomi. So the other lot must be heading there. You'll have to find out which party the stuff's with before you get there, so you'll know whether to stick with the religiosos or trail the rest at a distance."

"How long will I have?"

"God knows. Several days. They don't exactly break speed records.... But, if you ask me, it'll be with the other lot – the traders and such. Pilgrims travel light. It will be easier to conceal a heavy lead canister among bundles of merchandise on pack camels than it would be among bedrolls and riders."

"True. But I have to be sure. After all, they do have a specific place to take it, don't they?"

"Isn't Gabotomi one of the so-called Forbidden Cities?" Illya asked suddenly.

"Was, old boy. Was. It's in the middle of the rebel country now. You chaps are heading for a hotbed of trouble, you know."

"Yes, what's the strength of this rebel bit?" Solo queried.

"Strong enough, actually. Of course they play it down up here. But in fact there's a spot of the old genocide going on in the south. Real race-war stuff. Up here and in the Nile Valley and the desert, it's all arabs; the Muslims rule the country, after all. But the uncivilized part, in the south – that's all missionary Christians, fetichists and so on. And of course they loathe each other's guts. As soon as the Raj pulled out, the arabs began a systematic campaign of wiping out the others. They send troops down and wipe out whole villages – kill the lot and burn the places to the ground.... So naturally the natives consider themselves a persecuted minority, and to be an arab in that area is to be a dead man. If you have to leave that caravan, Mr Solo, I should junk those borrowed robes pretty dam' quick! You can't trust those types, you know."

59

"One can see where your own sympathies lie," Solo said.

"With the arabs, you mean? Well, of course – I mean, well, you *can* talk to them, can't you?"

After dark, when the fierce and breathless heat of the day had abated, they paid their bill and checked out of the hotel. Illya was to fly to Stanleyville in the Congo, from where – if Waverly had acted on Marshel's radioed request – a helicopter would take him north to the Sudan border. Here, he was to move north farther still, assume the role of a big game photographer, and move into the Sudan in a Landrover.

"We'll keep in touch by radio," Solo said. "If you prospect in the general direction of Gabotomi and Halakaz, and keep your eyes and ears open, you might come across something. Good God, if they're building an atomic plant or hydrogen bombs, something must be there to see; *somebody* must have noticed. Those places take up acres and acres! ... In the meantime, I'll stick with the caravan and try to trail the canister. With luck, we ought to end up at the same place...."

As soon as Kuryakin had left for the airport with most of their equipment, he himself hurried to a rendezvous with a man called Nassim. Under Rodney Marshel's guidance, he suffered himself to be stained brown all over and bearded, hair by hair, along the edge of his jawline. His teeth were discoloured, his hands roughened and his nails artificially cracked and grimed. With wax cunningly inserted inside his nostrils to alter the shape of his nose, he would have passed unrecognized even by Waverly....

"According to your papers, *effendi*," Nassim said, stepping back to admire his handiwork, "you have come all the way from Al Khuraiba in Saudi Arabia to go on this pilgrimage. Let us hope this will be considered sufficient excuse for any inconsistencies of accent when you speak arabic!"

Beneath the heavy burnous, Solo slung the borrowed Mauser in a makeshift holster which Marshel had provided. Around his waist, next to the skin, was a Chubb-locked money belt – containing, apart from local currencies, his miniature transmitter-receiver and one or two other devices.

Then, with Nassim as his guide, he mounted a horse and rode out of the city towards the dawn rendezvous which was to begin his uncomfortable journey into the unknown....

CHAPTER EIGHT

CAVEAT FOR THE GENERAL

THE frontier was a collection of wooden huts straddling the dust road; the border was a barbed wire fence interrupted by a striped pole with a counterweight on one end. Inside the hut nearest to the highway, a platoon of soldiers lounged, exchanging pleasantries with the frontier guards. Soldiers and guards wore British-style khaki uniforms – and all of the men there were Africans.

Illya slid the Landrover to a halt in a cloud of dust and climbed out on to the road. Something had gone wrong with the arrangements. There had been no helicopter at Stanleyville, nor was there any message from Waverly or anyone else in New York. U.N.C.L.E. had no representative in the town and there was nobody he could trust well enough to send a radio message. Solo was out of range of the miniature transmitter. Accordingly, the Russian had played it by ear and hired his own vehicle. The 450 mile drive had taken him three days, and now, when Solo was traversing the high ridge between the basins of the Nile and the Bahr-el-Ghaza and Illya himself should have been prospecting the environs of Gabotomi, he was only just entering the country. . . .

Perspiration clogged his fair hair and trickled between his shoulder blades as he tramped across the blazing forecourt to the guard hut. In three hours it would be dark, yet it was still tremendously hot.

A tall African, carrying the three stripes of a sergeant, deliberated over Kuryakin's papers. Then he glanced over the Russian's shoulder, stiffened and snapped out a parade-ground salute. Illya swung round. Although the face was so dark, his first impression of the man he now faced was of all brightness and light. The Sam Browne crossing his compact chest gleamed; the riding boots winked in the sun; the insignia of a Major-General shone from his shoulder tabs; and from under his arm the silver-knobbed head of a cane glistened. Brilliantly white teeth flashed between thick lips as the cane reached out to touch the papers on the trestle table.

"And what have we here, sergeant?" he asked. "A foreigner seeking entry?" The voice was deep and mellifluous, overlaid with a caricature of an Oxford accent.

"Yes, sir."

The smile turned through sixty degrees and beamed on Illya. "Edmond Mazzari," the voice continued. "Officer commanding troops rightfully in charge of this region. May one ask your reasons for wishing to enter the Sudan at this particular point?"

"Good afternoon, General," Illya said. "The answer is simple: I am a photographer of animals. Certain of the beasts I wish to photograph can only be found in the area."

"For example?"

"Certain types of white rhino; cave baboons; elephant; tiger; various members of the deer family."

"But all these, my dear fellow, can be found in other parts of Africa – rhinoceros, elephant, tigers. We have no monopoly of them, you know."

"In game preserves, yes. Shabby, half tame creatures with threadbare hides. What I want are photographs of *wild* animals – and not the stereotyped pictures of a blurred rhino charging or a lion hanging its head by a water hole. I am prepared to wait for what I want. I have patience. What I seek are records of these animals behaving believably *as* animals, as creatures of a family, as hunters, as beasts in fear – not just another series of myths from a child's geography book."

"It would be an approach long due," the General said. "What camera are you proposing to use for these pictures, Mr . . . ?"

"Kuryakin." Illya snapped open the leather case at his side.

"Ah. A Hasselblad. With all the extras. Do you know, old chap, that the money that camera would bring could feed one of my villages in there for a month?" He stabbed the cane towards the rolling savanna across the frontier.

"I know that things in this region are – difficult," Kuryakin said equivocally.

"Difficult! If I were to tell you . . . Do you realize, old chap, that the arabs in the north are engaged in a war of extermination down here? They're systematically killing my people off. Every day they descend on another village and – pouff!" He shouldered the cane like a rifle and shot down an imaginary adversary.

"I did not know it was as bad as that. To be honest, though, I was surprised not to find arab troops guarding this frontier post."

"There were. Yesterday." The General swung his stick towards a row of freshly turned mounds of soil behind one of the huts. "We show the flag occasionally – just to emphasize our rights, you know. These good fellows" – he pointed at the guard hut – "will stay here until another troop descend on them. There will be another little skirmish – and another row of graves on our African soil. Then we will take another post . . ."

"Forgive my ignorance, but what is the background to this?"

"Nothing but arab rapacity. Basically, of course, it's religious on their side. Our people here in the south are Christians or pagans; they are Musselmen – muscle men! That's good, eh? – and so we have to go. We would have accepted some kind of federation if only we had been allowed a say in governing our own three provinces. But too many in Khartoum do nothing but line their own pockets – and mouth promises they have no intention of keeping. And anyway, we shall accept nothing less than secession after what they have done now."

"It's very bad, is it?"

"Bad?" Mazzari had a trick of repeating the last word uttered by his *vis-a-vis*. "It is so bad as to be unbelievable. The arab officers quartered here are in fear of their lives, so they lounge about in the towns and leave their troops to burn and loot and murder as they will. Do you realize, old chap, that they have destroyed – completely eradicated – one hundred and thirty-three villages here and in southeastern Sudan? They have murdered more than thirty thousand people, leaving the survivors to wander in the bush and starve. In the last two years, such murders, plus disease, starvation and a drain of refugees fleeing across the borders, has reduced our population by over a million. A million, Mr Kuryakin. That is one third of our African population down here...."

"Isn't there quite a strong underground movement – the Anya Nya, I believe?" Illya said, at a loss for anything more suitable to say.

"The Anya Nya? Lazzaro is a skilled guerilla leader: but he has one bazooka and a handful of rifles among a few thousand irregulars, over there to the east in the Dongotona Mountains. What can such groups do against the fifteen thousand heavily armed arabs in the region? Could they prevent the Juba massacre in the summer of 1965, when fourteen hundred people were killed in a single night? They fight in bowler hats and shorts!" The General was contemptuous.

"And here...?"

"Here in the southwest, we order things better. A little better, old chap. The Nya Nyerere – the force I command – is six thousand strong; but armed, disciplined and efficient."

"I can see that," Kuryakin said, glancing at Mazzari's Sandhurst-style turnout.

"But today numbers are nothing. Efficiency is next to nothing. It is weapons that count – and the men that know how to use them. Soon, very soon, the Nya Nyerere will be as sixty thousand men – as six million. And then the arab politicians in Khartoum will bewail their fate. We shall grind the oppressors into the dust and become masters of the whole Sudan." For a moment, Oxford University went out the window and in its place pure mission school showed through.

"You are planning a *coup*, General?" Illya strove not to betray his interest.

"Ah, it's early days; early days, old chap," General Mazzari said, conscious that he had revealed perhaps a little too much. "Just keep your eyes on the headlines in a few weeks time, that's all. In the meantime, we *are* still an underground army. I must be off."

"I have your permission to proceed?"

"So far as I am concerned, you may go ahead and take your animal pictures. But I can offer no guarantee for your safety. You would be wise to stay the minimum amount of time – and keep your eyes wide open. *Caveat emptor*, old chap. *Caveat emptor!*"

He snapped his cane back under his arm, saluted, and strode smartly from the hut.

The guards raised the pole; Illya climbed wearily back into the Landrover and drove on. For fifteen or twenty miles, the rolling grassland continued. Then the clumps of trees grew farther and farther apart, the herds of antelope vanished, the grasses became thin – and soon the trail was twisting up into the desolate foothills of a range of mountains that had showed as a blue smudge on the horizon at the border.

Three times he passed the burned-out shells of African villages, only a ring of scorched earth and a few crumbling mud walls remaining to show where they had been. The one sign of cultivation was a ragged line of corn by the roadside that had gone to seed. The route grew steeper, dipping every now and then into a rubble of stones and rocks in a dried-up river bed, and then mounting again towards the saddle which pierced the limestone cliffs topping the ridge.

Once through the pass, Illya found himself descending to an upland plain – a featureless wilderness of thorny scrub broken at intervals by tangles of huge boulders. He would have to make camp for the night soon; the heat had already gone from the air and the sun was dropping out of sight behind the crest of the mountains. He pulled up and switched off the Landrover's engine. After the continual whining of low gear and the boom of the exhaust, it was very quiet. Wind rattled the spikes of the thorn trees beside the road.

He spread out a map. Two hundred miles farther on, the road led to Wau, in Bahr-el-Ghazal province. Ninety miles before that, there was a fork, where he would take the right-hand trail for Halakaz – and after that he was on his own; for there were no roads to Gabatomi, nor was it marked on the map. . . .

The Russian shivered and restarted the motor. He

couldn't face the idea of spending the night in this Godforsaken place. But when night fell with tropical suddenness an hour later, he was still driving through the interminable scrub. To drive with headlights would make him visible for fifty miles. Reluctantly, he turned off the road and parked the vehicle out of sight behind a pile of flat rocks.

He opened one of the baggage rolls in the back and ate. Then, wrapping himself in blankets, he settled down as comfortably as he could in the offside passenger seat and tried to sleep. Beside him, in the Landrover's central seat, lay a heavy calibre automatic – the nucleus of the special U.N.C.L.E. gun which had been developed at a cost of one thousand dollars each. On to it could be screwed four attachments: a shoulder stock, a rifle barrel, an extension to the butt, and a telescopic sight – the completed device producing a spidery-looking weapon of great fire power and versatility.

For a long time, he huddled there in wakefulness, listening to a family of baboons coughing and chattering uneasily somewhere in the rocks above him. He could hear the occasional scuttling noise made by a prowling jerboa, the desert rat which somehow eked out an existence in the wilderness.

He would have liked to call up Solo on the radio – but the agent had asked him to keep radio silence until he himself called: the bleep of the receiver might attract attention in the caravan. His progress report, and the problem of the inexplicable absence of news from Waverly, would have to wait. At last he fell into a fitful sleep – to awake what seemed an age later, shivering with cold. He pulled another blanket from the roll and looked at the illuminated face of his watch: it was still only a quarter past ten. . . .

By midnight he was asleep again. But he awoke finally before dawn and waited in a fury of impatience for the sun to rise. It was still extremely cold. Moisture had penetrated the perspex side-screens, beading the dashboard instruments and controls and chilling him to the marrow.

He flung off the blankets, clambered stiffly to the ground, and stamped up and down on the barren earth, trying to restore his circulation and bring some warmth back into his body. The baboons chattered with anger and swung away over the top of the rocks.

The sky was becoming visible at last – a dirty grey expanse tinged with saffron above the scrub to the east. Slowly the mountains he had crossed the previous evening assembled themselves in undulations of purple and ultramarine. By the time the sun eventually jerked into sight above a charcoal-coloured cloudbank, Illya was already in the driving seat with the ignition key inserted.

But the Landrover was reluctant to start. The extremes of heat and cold had made the engine temperamental. Fearing that he might exhaust the battery, he got out again and swung it with the handle.

At his fifth attempt, the motor caught. He scrambled back inside and blipped the accelerator for a few minutes to warm up the engine compartment and chase the moisture from contacts and leads. Then, bumping over the stony ground, he steered slowly round the rocks and back on to the road. He stared.

Strung out across it in two lines, barring his progress in either direction, were a score of African soldiers armed with Belgian FN automatic rifles.

CHAPTER NINE

A QUESTION OF IDENTITY

WADI ELMIRA was a jumble of flat-roofed, mud-walled buildings; it spilled down the side of a valley gashed at the bottom by a stony ravine. At the foot of the ravine a trickle of brown water, later to become a tributary of the Bahr-el-Ghaza river, slid among the rocks. The caravan reached the place at nightfall, passing through the arched gate in the walls and turning aside soon afterwards to halt in a wide, open space before a domed mosque.

As soon as the beasts had been fed and watered, most of the members of the caravan plunged into the narrow streets of the town. Only the pilgrims, sitting quietly among their bedrolls, the women, and some old men were left under the date palms in the dusk. When the train split into two portions the following morning, each was to be escorted by a squadron of Sudanese cavalry, so it was more than ever important that Solo should locate the canister that night and identify the camel carrying it. Tomorrow might be too late.

For a while he debated with himself whether he should stay as he was or conduct his researches in different clothes. He was stuck with the facial disguise, for he would never be able to reapply it once it was removed. So far as garments went, a burnous would undoubtedly help him to remain anonymous; on the other hand it would restrict his movements if he was spotted and might lead any pursuers back to the caravan. . . .

Eventually he decided to dispense with it. He had erected his bivouac close by a crumbling wall which bordered one side of the open space where they were camped. The pack camels were lying near the tethered horses, some way beyond the trees on the far side. Inside the low tent, he wriggled out of the head-dress and robes, drawing on a pair of khaki shorts and a bush shirt. He was wearing rubber-soled sneakers. The Mauser was too conspicuous, he decided, and would have to be left behind.

Cautiously lifting the back flap of the bivouac, he crawled out and stood between tent and wall, listening. From somewhere over the rooftops reflected light from naphtha flares flickered, and there sounded a gabble of voices from the bazaars. Nearer at hand in the darkness, only an occasional murmured conversation and the movement of tethered beasts broke the silence.

It was now or never. Flexing his knees, he sprang lightly upwards and grasped the top of the wall. A moment later, he had hauled himself up and dropped to an evil-smelling alley choked with refuse on the far side.

He ran swiftly along the lane between the wall and the backs of a row of mean houses. A hundred yards farther on, the passage twisted away from the square around the bulk of the mosque and eventually emerged into a narrow street.

Solo paused, looking up and down. To his right, the street led towards the hubbub and the bright lights of a market place; to the left, it curved away into shadows. If he were to turn left, and left again somewhere, he should be able to double back and reach the square on the far side from his bivouac. He turned and hurried on.

There were many people in the street, most of them drifting towards the bazaar, but few gave more than a second look at the bearded arab in the bush shirt: the town was full of merchants, soldiers, refugees from the rebel country to the southwest, and country people in for the market.

Solo plunged down another alleyway to the left, squeezed past a veiled woman leading a donkey with bulging panniers, and ran on. Soon he was back in the square, crouched down behind the nearest line of recumbent camels. Fortunately, many of the traders in the caravan had unpacked their rolls to take samples to the bazaar, and to that extent his task was easier: the lead canister would be concealed somewhere in an untouched bale.

Furtively, crawling on hands and knees across the beaten earth between each camel, he searched and prodded and investigated with exploring fingers. After an hour he was half way along the third line of animals. The great beasts chewed noisily on the cud, turning their eyes to gaze incuriously at the crouching man. He was enveloped in the rank odour of their foetid breath.

Towards the end of the line, he fell forward as his wrist turned under him on a loose stone, and lurched against a bulging bale of merchandise still harnessed to a dromedary. The pack swung away from him in an odd manner. He saw that it didn't move as a tightly folded wad of materials should do. . . .

Feverishly, he turned towards it. In a moment, its secret was revealed. The thin layer of cloths on the outside was stretched over a wickerwork cage: inside, the bale was bulked out with some light substance like cotton wool -- and, buried in the centre, his fingers slid down the cold, greasy surface of a lead container.

He let out his breath in a long sigh. Unbuttoning the flap of his breast pocket, he drew out a small leather case containing two metal devices about the size of a matchbox. One of them emitted a continuous radio signal; with the dial of the other correctly tuned, one could trace the movements of the first device from a distance by following the direction in which the bleeps were the loudest.

For a moment he hesitated, wondering where to conceal the homing device. Its magnetic limpet attachment would be useless on lead. Finally, he shrugged and thrust it as far as he could into the cotton beneath the canister. At least now he would be able to keep track of the camel carrying the deadly load, even if he had to leave the caravan when the two portions split up. The homer had a range of over thirty miles.

Just in case, though . . . he permitted himself the briefest flash from a pencil flashlight. Between the bogus bale carrying the canister and the balancing pack on the animal's other side, he found a rolled blanket in yellow, red and black striped material. This would give him a visual check as well.

Carefully, he replaced the coverings over the wicker cage, tightened the retaining straps, and crawled back the way he had come. He was rising to his feet at the end of the line when a torchlight beam blazed at him from behind a tree trunk.

"What are you doing?" a harsh voice snarled. "Stay still or I shall shoot." There was a movement towards him in the shadows.

Solo froze. "Pardon," he said in French. "I was trying to find my way to the central bazaar. Perhaps Monsieur could direct me?"

"On your hands and knees? A likely story! Come here and let's have a good look at you. The police and the military here do not look too kindly on thefts from caravans." The man with the torch advanced. It was Ahmed, the camel-master.

Solo went slowly forward, thankful that he had had the foresight to change clothes. "I assure you, Monsieur, that there was no question of theft," he said. "I had lost my way and I fell. When you saw me, I was just rising again..."

"We shall see about that," the other sneered. "Put up your hands and we shall find out what you have stolen."

The agent raised his arms, and kept still. Ahmed came closer, circling him warily, the barrel of a revolver gleaming in the light from the torch. He patted Solo on both hips and under the arms, running his fingers expertly up the inside of his thighs and across his stomach.

"At least you're not armed," he said. "That should get the sentence reduced by perhaps five years – Aha! What have we here?" His hand had touched the hard bulge of the leather case in Solo's breast pocket.

"A transistor radio," Solo said truthfully.

"I shall believe that when I see it. Let's have it."

"You want me to take it out?"

"Quick." The gun jabbed Solo hard in the small of the back.

He lowered his right arm slowly and unbuttoned the flap of the pocket, drawing out the case with the homer in it between finger and thumb. Then, before the exclamation of satisfaction had left Ahmed's lips, he dropped the case and his hand streaked down and behind him, knocking the other's gun arm aside. The heavy calibre revolver roared as Solo whirled and grasped the hand which held it in both of his own. He jerked the man's arm up and then down, exerting a paralysing judo grip on the wrist. When the barrel was pointing at the ground, the pistol exploded again,

72

the ricochet whining away among the trees from the stony terrain.

As the weapon finally dropped from his nerveless fingers, Ahmed slammed the heel of his other hand under Solo's chin, pushing back his head with agonizing force. Solo went with the thrust, letting go the man's wrist and rolling backwards. At the same time, he brought up his knees, lodged his heels in Ahmed's crutch and then suddenly straightened his legs. The camel-master flew over his head and crashed to the ground behind him with a clatter which echoed around the square.

In a flash, Solo was on his feet and running towards the alley by which he had entered the place. This was no time for a prolonged combat: all that mattered was that he should get away and back to his tent before he was recognized. Aroused by the shots, people were already running towards them from the encampment.

Pausing only to scoop up the leather case he had dropped and boot the revolver into the shadows, he dashed for the corner. Before he reached it, Ahmed was shouting abuse at him as he scrambled after the gun. A moment later a third shot rang out. The wind of the bullet fanned Solo's left shoulder. Then he was around the corner and pelting down the alley towards the street which led to the bazaar.

Before he reached the second corner, he stopped abruptly and melted into the shadows of a doorway. Half a dozen soldiers with drawn pistols clattered into the alley from the street and ran past him towards the sounds of the confused shouting in the square.

Once they had gone, Solo slid out of his hiding place and walked rapidly away from the noise. "But you *must* have passed him," he could hear Ahmed furiously calling as he turned the corner. "He ran down that passage only a few seconds before you arrived...."

The agent joined the throng which moved towards the bazaar and strove to conceal the fact that he was hurrying. Arab women veiled in black, *fellaheen* in striped shifts and tarbooshes, peasants in rags and Bedouin in flowing white robes jostled against him as he walked. Somewhere in the crowd behind him, he could sense, there was an eddying and a commotion as Ahmed and the soldiers ran back into the street. Dimly over the general noise he could hear voices raised in argument and shouts of protest.

In the market place, the shuffling of feet was drowned in the cries of barkers and the traditional haggling of merchants and customers. Hands gesticulated, fingers wagged, palms were upraised in the suffocating press among the stalls of fruit, vegetables, cloth and hardware under the flares.

He had almost shouldered his way through to the far side when three shots rang out above the heads of the crowd. There was a screaming and a stampede as everybody fought to get away from the centre of the market. A great stand of copper pots and pans near Solo careened over as half a dozen robed arabs forced their way between two stalls.

". . . where you are. Don't leave the market place!" a voice shouted over the clangour of falling hardware and the furious protests of the stallholder. "There is a foreign thief at large here and we want to find him. This is the military. Stay where you are – you have nothing to fear."

Feeling as though he had suddenly been exposed in the glare of a searchlight, Solo slunk round behind the stall and made for a street twisting away into the shadows. If he was to go a hundred yards down there and then find a right turn, he might be able to circle round and find the lane which led to the wall sheltering his bivouac.

"Over there!" another voice was shouting. "Look – on the far side of the bazaar. Quick! After him!"

He glanced over his shoulder. The owner of the hardware stall, his arms full of saucepans, was dancing up and down and pointing towards him. Beyond, advancing rapidly down a lane between the striped awnings, Ahmed and the soldiers came running.

He himself broke into a run and plunged down the dark street. A fusillade of shots erupted behind him as he gained the shadows. Bullets spurted the dust on either side of his pounding feet; another chipped plaster from the wall by his shoulder.

Solo hared round the first bend in the street. There was no turning off to the right. The roadway led towards the lights of another square. He dashed into an entry on the left, ran up a flight of stone stairs, crossed a wider street and plunged through an archway into a maze of unlit alleyways. Behind him, the footsteps and voices of the hunters approached. There had been plenty of people in the street he had crossed to point out the way he had gone.

He pressed on, down a second flight of steps, and found himself in a narrow lane which had street lamps at dim intervals. All around him a faint murmuration of voices behind closed shutters stirred the warm air. Music rose and fell in the distance.

He halted, panting.

"Why do you not come inside, stranger?" a soft voice intoned in arabic at his elbow.

He swung round. There was a click. In the upward-directed beam of a small flashlight, brown flesh quivered. The small circle of illumination revealed the upper half of a girl's body. Below a tight swathe of diaphanous material sheathed the shoulders. Above, the gleam of teeth, the highlight on a full lip, shone through the shadows.

Solo hesitated. The sounds of pursuit were only one corner away. Already feet were scrambling down the steps.

"Alright," he said huskily, making up his mind. He stepped towards the doorway. The light vanished. A door creaked open into darkness.

Solo brushed past the girl and stood waiting as she closed the door. In the airless dark of the passage, the perfume of some exotic, cloying cosmetic washed over him. Outside, footsteps scraped to a halt. He could hear the voice of Ahmed: " . . . A foreigner. Medium height, bearded, and wearing western clothes."

Somebody mumbled a negative.

"But he must be here somewhere. He can't have got away! . . . I've seen the bastard before somewhere, but for the moment I just can't place him. There's something familiar about him all the same. . . ."

"He could be anywhere here," another voice chimed in. "You know where we are? This is the street of – "

"It doesn't matter what street it is," a third voice, clipped and commanding, interrupted. "We'll post sentries at either end and search it house by house." The footsteps moved away decisively.

The girl, whose breath had hissed in sharply the first time Ahmed spoke, now moved past Solo towards the back of the building. Soft flesh brushed his bare arm. She said in a low voice: "This way. I will show you. . . ."

Light stabbed the blackness as she switched on the torch and shone the beam at the floor behind her to light the way. Solo followed her to the end of the passage and up a flight of stone stairs. Apart from the clip-clop of the girl's slippers and the swish of garments against her flanks, they mounted in silence. At the top of the stairs a dimly lit foyer appeared with a number of doors off it.

The girl opened one and walked into a tiny room of about eight feet square, furnished with nothing more than rugs and cushions upon the floor. As she crossed to draw heavy drapes across an arched window embrasure, Solo closed the door silently and leaned against it. "I am sorry," he began, "I only want to. . . ."

For the first time, the girl turned to face him. It was Yemanja – the belly dancer from the caravan who had been giving him the come-on throughout the journey.

"So," she said softly. "It is you!"

"Yemanja! I didn't recognize you. I – "

"Why would you, my friend? How could you recognize that which you will not see? . . . But *I* recognize *you* – although evidently Ahmed does not . . . yet."

"I do not wish you to misunderstand me, Yemanja. When I came in here – "

"I know. If you had recognized me, you would have run away; the way you always run away with your eyes when I look at you. Why do you rebuff me, my friend? Am I not beautiful? Am I not desirable?" The girl sank down on a pile of cushions, staring at him with her enormous eyes.

"You are very beautiful," Solo said, "and very desirable. I swear it."

"Then . . . ?"

The agent hesitated. Dare he trust the girl? If she had taken such a fancy to him, it might be worth the risk. On the other hand, a woman scorned . . . Mentally, he shrugged. He really had no choice.

"I am engaged upon a certain mission," he said carefully. "In order to complete this successfully, it is vital that I do not in any way attract attention while I am with the caravan."

"So? You are running away, are you not? It was you that Ahmed and the soldiers were chasing, no? Evidently you are on some secret business, for you are dressed as an *effendi*. But this is no concern of mine. Why do you not stay here with me? Come – sit here beside me and I will send for some refreshment."

"Yemanja, I cannot."

"But I wish it. You are beautiful. You have a kind and gentle face. You are different, my friend. In my life I have not met men like you. If you find me pleasing, why do you reject me?"

"If I . . . become friendly . . . with you, it will make Ahmed jealous. And if he becomes more jealous than he already is, he will notice me all the more in the caravan – and that must not happen; because, you see, he does not yet connect the man he is chasing tonight with the man his woman so obviously likes in the caravan."

"Ahmed!" The girl's voice was full of scorn. "He is a brute, that one. He beats me. Look – I will show you. . . ."

"No, no," Solo said hastily. "I believe you."

"Anyway, I wish to leave him. I do not understand this of the caravan and your private business. I have said it does not concern me. You need not be afraid of Ahmed: he is a bully, all brag and no courage."

"I am not afraid of him. It is just that he must not notice me."

"Well, he *cannot* notice you here," the girl cried triumphantly.

She broke off abruptly. From somewhere below a persistent hammering came echoing up the stairway.

Yemanja rose on to her knees, her eyes wide with alarm. "The soldiers," she whispered. "They said they would search every house. . . ."

"Oh, no! Not again!" Solo said in English.

"You are right, my friend. They must not find you here. You must go."

"Yes, but how?"

"Nobody saw you come in. So far as they know, I have been here alone all the time. If you leave through this window...."

"Does Ahmed know you are here?"

"Of course. I am here at his command. Where do you wish to go?"

"I want to get back to a lane which runs behind the wall at one side of the square where the encampment is."

The girl drew back the curtain over the window embrasure. "Out here is a flat roof. Beyond is an alley. You cannot get back directly without crossing the street in front here. So take the alley in the opposite direction and you will find you are in the street circling the town inside the walls. Turn right along this and you will find that the – one, two, three, four, yes, fifth – the fifth turning will lead you to the mosque. And from there, the lane you speak of – "

"Yes, yes. I know the way from there," Solo said. The hammering had stopped and there was the sound of many voices below. He swung a leg over the window sill, and then turned back towards the girl.

"You are very beautiful and very kind," he said. "I am grateful. If ever there is anything I can do...."

"You know what you can do," the girl said.

Solo grinned, leaned inwards and kissed her briefly on the lips. The next instant she was all over him, devouring him with kisses, her body pressed against his chest, her hands cradling, caressing the back of his head. Gently, he disengaged himself.

"The soldiers," he reminded her in a whisper.

"I had not forgotten. But I will not forget you, either. You will see me again, my friend. I am a determined woman...."

Solo waved and jumped lightly on to the flat roof. The curtain slid back over the window.

The drop to the alley was about fifteen feet. Even in his rubber-soled sneakers, he seemed to himself to make quite a noise when he landed. But nobody appeared to have heard; no voice questioned him and no footsteps advanced. After waiting a moment, listening, he ran lightly off in the direction the girl had suggested.

The beaten earth road inside the wall of the town was deserted. Just before he got to the fifth turning, he saw the back of a patrolling sentry silhouetted against the sky on top of the wall. But he had reached the safety of the corner before the man had reached the end of his beat.

The mosque was nearly a quarter of a mile down the quiet street. There was one dangerous spot, when he had to cross an open space between the end of the street and the domed building – but the few passers-by were all facing towards the lights of the bazaar, which showed through an archway on the far side. Shouts of command from the soldiers could still be heard above the hubbub of the market.

Solo passed noiselessly behind the watchers and turned the corner of the mosque. Two minutes later, he was jumping for the top of the wall which bounded the encampment. Peering cautiously over the top, he saw that he had overestimated the distance by about two yards. He dropped back into the lane and climbed up again behind his bivouac. Then, lowering himself quietly behind the tent, he lifted the back flap and crawled inside with a sigh of relief.

As soon as he had stripped off the bush shirt and shorts and resumed the burnous, he looked out across the square from the front. Flares had been set up where the beasts were tethered. One of the horses was restive, snorting and rearing on the end of its rope. A group of soldiers lounged by the entrance to the alleyway down which he had made his escape, and, nearer at hand, Ahmed paced up and down with a tall, dark man in arab robes.

"I don't see how he *can* have got away," the camelmaster was saying angrily. "We had the whole street bottled up. . . . I don't think it likely, but just in case he did come from here, I am asking the soldiers to arouse all these people" – he gestured towards the corner of the encampment where Solo and the other pilgrims were quartered – "and get them out so we can have a look at them."

The tall man took his arm. "It is not necessary," he said. "There are plans, my friends, of which you know nothing. Leave it."

Solo withdrew like a tortoise into his bivouac and rolled himself in his sleeping bag. Ten minutes later, he was asleep.

CHAPTER TEN

THE RETREAT OF NAPOLEON

THE rendezvous with the cavalry was outside the south gate of Wadi Elmira. From here, the pilgrims continued along the left bank of the river, while the pack train negotiated a ford and climbed up into the hills on the right.

Napoleon Solo kept his head well down as Ahmed rode up and down the long line of camels and horses with a Sudanese officer, separating the travellers and their beasts into two sections. The dromedary with the red, yellow and black striped blanket roll was one of a string of three led by a paunchy Bedouin immediately behind the head of the column. The camel-master's heavy features were set in their usual scowl as he manoeuvred his horse in among the throng of riders, roughly shepherding them into the correct line.

Solo kneed his camel as unobtrusively as he could towards the file of pilgrims, hoping to escape notice while Ahmed's back was turned. But the army officer saw him move and called out: "Hey! You, there! Where do you think you're going?" He spurred his horse towards the agent, cursing freely. Fortunately Ahmed was disputing some point with a burly pilgrim and did not accompany him.

"I was but joining my fellow pilgrims," Solo said meekly, as the soldier reined up beside him.

"You wait until you are told. And that is a strange manner in which you speak, my friend," the officer said.

"My speech is not as yours by virtue of the fact that I have travelled far," the agent said. "I come from Al Khuraiba in Saudi Arabia."

"H'mm. Well, see that you do not get out of line again." The cavalryman wheeled his mount and rejoined Ahmed.

When his turn came, Solo showed his papers with bent head and suffered himself to be pushed into the line of pilgrims. The camel with the striped blanket, as he had expected, was with the other train.

A few minutes later, the pilgrims and their escort moved off along the river bank while the baggage train with its attendant squadron splashed across the ford and began climbing the rocky trail on the far side.

Solo deliberately lagged, hoping that he would have a chance to break away from the caravan and somehow rejoin the other train undetected. After a half mile, his chance came: the trail wound through a twisting gorge, and all the escorting soldiers were up at the head of the column. He reined in his beast behind a group of enormous boulders and allowed the others to move slowly around the corner out of sight. Then, turning about, he rode back up the trail as fast as the camel would go.

Fording the river, he urged the animal on up the steep path the baggage train had followed. The road mounted steadily past tiny cultivated squares, planted with millet, maize and sorgho, through a belt of trees, and across an exposed slope of bare rock, where it turned unexpectedly to the right and followed a dried-up valley towards the crest of the ridge.

A huge natural tunnel through the porous limestone led beneath the ridge itself – and on the far side he could see, far down the slope, the long line of horses and camels he was trying to join. If he could manage to link up with the caravan without being noticed, there was a slim chance that he could stay with it at least until nightfall.

The track – although it was dry – produced very little dust from the passage of the camel's feet. He rode on down, steering his swaying mount behind the shelter of every rock outcrop and pile of boulders that the terrain offered.

An hour later, he was within a quarter of a mile of the caravan. Clearly around the bends in the trail he could hear the sounds of its progress. He took the chance to close up when the route began to follow a tortuous path between an alternating series of dried-up alluvial deposits. If only there were no cavalrymen riding at the back when he tagged on, he prayed.

But when he rounded the last corner and caught up, he saw that his luck had changed: two horsemen in uniform were riding behind the last pack camel.

Before he had time to withdraw, one of them turned round and saw him. There wasn't a chance of escape. The men were carrying rifles across their cruppers; besides, a horse could run rings around a camel, in a race. Fuming inwardly, he rode straight ahead until he caught up with them.

"What the devil do you think you are doing?" the man who had seen him said roughly. "Show me your papers at once."

While the other soldier kept him covered, Solo reached inside the folds of his robe and produced the documents. "But you should be with the other train!" the soldier exclaimed. "Who are you? and what are you doing here?"

"I missed my way. I was wandering about, lost, when I heard the sound of your caravan and thought it might be the one I missed – "

"Impossible. The others are miles away, on the other side of the river. You couldn't have got here by mistake. Here, Ali: ride up to the front of the column and fetch Ahmed and the Captain while I keep an eye on this man."

The second cavalryman spurred his horse and rode after the disappearing caravan while Solo remained motionless under the other's watchful guard. In a few minutes, four horsemen galloped into sight round a bend in the trail: the soldier, Ahmed, the officer who had spoken to Solo before the trains had separated, and a tall, dark man on a splendid grey mount – the stranger Solo had seen talking to Ahmed in the square the previous night.

"What is the trouble?" the dark man asked curtly.

"This man was attempting to join the train, Excellence."

"But I have seen him before," the officer said. "I had trouble with him when we were separating the two caravans."

"So have I seen him before," Ahmed snarled. "I knew the face was familiar!" He leaned across and twitched the enveloping head-dress the agent wore. "Aha! So the foreign thief is revealed – foreign thief . . . and, perhaps, foreign spy, eh?"

The cavalry captain looked enquiringly at the dark man. "I suppose so," the latter sighed. "It was planned otherwise –

but, in the circumstances... At least, it seems we now know the mystery of the radio transmissions from the caravan. We can search his baggage afterwards." He nodded imperceptibly at the officer.

"Get down," the captain ordered Solo curtly.

The agent slid from the dromedary, his mind racing. The homer and his tiny two-way radio were safe in the money belt around his waist; the Mauser was in its improvised holster under his robes; and on his other side was slung a pair of powerful binoculars. The rest of his gear would have to be sacrificed along with the bedroll on the camel... assuming he could get away at all. Unobtrusively, he grasped the big automatic through a fold in his burnous.

As his feet touched the ground, Solo heard the chilling sound of a rifle bolt being drawn back and slammed home. He knew that he was very near to death: the soldier behind him was preparing to shoot....

Exploding into motion, he ducked under the camel's belly and fired at the cavalryman through his robes. The soldier toppled forward over his horse's neck, his rifle clattering to the ground. Before any of the others had time to move, Solo bobbed up on the far side of the animal and the Mauser roared again. The second man, winged in the act of raising his rifle, clutched at his shoulder and sagged in his saddle.

An instant later, in a smooth, continuous flow of motion, the agent had bounded across the space between the camel and the first soldier's horse, hauled the dead man clear of the harness and vaulted into the saddle. Then, driving his heels into the animal's flanks, he rode straight at Ahmed, the officer and the stranger, scattering them before they could draw their guns, leaped the horse over a four-foot thorn hedge by the side of the trail, and galloped away into the scrub.

From behind him, Ahmed's revolver boomed. The report was followed by the sharp crack of an automatic and a duller, flatter explosion – probably someone had snatched up a rifle from one of the fallen soldiers.

Solo rode like the wind, zigzagging among the stunted trees. He was thankful that the soldier's horse – unlike most arab steeds – was harnessed and saddled. Crouching low over the animal's flying mane, he glanced back over his shoulder.

Ahmed and the officer had jumped the hedge and were galloping in pursuit; the dark man had stayed behind. His head and shoulders were visible over the line of thorn bushes, one eye squinting along the barrel of a rifle. Four more shots rang out. Then for a long time there was no sound but the drumming of hooves on the hard ground.

The agent was making a big circle through the scrub, trying to come back on a course parallel with the trail but about a mile away from it. He hoped to gain a range of low hills some way ahead and keep watch on the caravan for as long as he could before relying on the homer. In the meantime, there was the pursuit to be left behind.

Next time he looked back Ahmed had dropped half a mile behind – but the cavalry officer was only about a hundred yards away and gaining fast. There was a puff of smoke and a bullet sang over Solo's head.

Regretfully, the agent fumbled inside his robes until he reached the money belt. From a back compartment, he drew out a small, lozenge-shaped metal object about the size of a stud-box. As he rode, he twisted a pointer on the face to the mark *5 seconds*. Then, deliberately reining back a little, he waited for a straight stretch between the thorn trees and dropped the thing to the ground. The Sudanese was firing again – but after three shots a heavier detonation roared out and drowned the noise of horses' hooves as the grenade Solo had dropped went off.

He looked behind him again. Horse and rider were lying in a grotesque tangle among the trees. The bare earth, and parts of some of the tree trunks, glistened redly in the mounting sun.

Half an hour later, Solo reined in the horse between two monolithic rocks on the crest of the range of hills he had previously seen. From the shadows he watched through his binoculars as the caravan wound its way around the far end of the spur on which he stood. The camel with the striped blanket still walked just behind the posse of cavalry at the head of the column. It would be twenty minutes or a half hour before the last riders passed the foot of the slope immediately below him.

He decided to rest the horse and call up Illya on the radio: he had not contacted him at all, and Kuyrakin must be wondering what had happened. Besides, he himself wanted to know how the Russian had fared on his journeying from the other direction.

Sheltered by the rocks from the fierce heat, he sat down, took out the transmitter and, turning the pointer to *receive*, pressed the button which actuated the automatic call sign on their wavelength.

At the end of the half hour – the last outriders of the caravan had passed below him some time before – he was still pressing it.

There was no reply from Kuryakin. . . .

CHAPTER ELEVEN

THE CITY WHICH WAS OFF THE MAP

THE receiver in Illya Kuryakin's breast pocket began to bleep after he had been arguing for nearly two hours with the officer in charge of the detachment of soldiers who had stopped him resuming his journey after his night in the Landrover.

Colonel Ononu was short and bulky, with fierce, bright eyes in a very dark face. He was a volatile man, speaking in a declamatory fashion and constantly throwing out his arms and then smoothing down the creases in his rumpled bush shirt and shorts. Every now and then he would snatch the French paratroop beret he wore from his head, as if to emphasize a point, and then cram it back again on top of his close-cropped hair. The issue between them was simple: Illya wanted to go on; the Colonel wanted him to go back. Either that or submit to arrest – for he was not entirely satisfied with the Russian's credentials, he said.

"What do you want to go for, man? What for?" Ononu said. "This is dangerous country. We got a civil war on our hands, man – you could say the whole place is under martial law. . . . Okay, technically the province is still ruled by the arabs. Technically, I say. But possession is nine tenths of the law, even martial law, and we're here . . . and we're in possession of *you*, man."

"Granted, granted, granted, Colonel," Illya said patiently. "For the tenth time, I have pictures to take: in my opinion the only place I am likely to get them is further on here – "

"Where further on? How far you goin'? There's nothing to take around here – unless you want shots of the villagers murdered by the arabs."

"As I said, I'm taking this road as far as the fork for Halakaz, and – according to my map – the Halakaz road crosses a range of volcanic mountains and then skirts an enormous forest before it reaches the town a hundred miles further on. There are no roads through the forest – indeed, I understand it is hardly explored at all, and certainly not by Europeans. And it is here that I hope to be able to get the animal photos I want."

The Colonel flung out his arms in a theatrical gesture. "Pictures, animals, photographs!" he cried. "I tell you there's a race war going on here, man! You'd do better to photograph some of the atrocities – "

At this moment the call sign on Illya's radio began sounding insistently.

"What's that?" Ononu demanded suspiciously.

"A transistor radio," Kuryakin said innocently. "I must have left it on . . ."

"Give it to me."

"But it's my personal property . . ."

"There's no personal property in a war, man," the Colonel exclaimed, dragging off his beret and slapping his thigh with it. "When will you Europeans realize that this is *Africa*? Give it to me, I say."

As one of the ring of soldiers surrounding them moved a step forward, jerking up the barrel of his automatic rifle, the agent drew the radio reluctantly from his pocket and handed it over. Ononu dropped the red beret back on his head and examined the compact device, turning it over and over in his hands. As the bleeping continued, a hot, dry wind stirred eddies in the dust at their feet and agitated the stiletto-like spikes of the thorn trees.

"But this is not a music radio," the Colonel said at last. "This is a talking radio. Somebody is talking to you, calling you. Who?"

"My partner."

"Partner? What is his name? Where is he?"

"His name is Waverly," Illya said easily. "He is supposed to be somewhere up in the forest area already. He is probably calling me to say that he has found a suitable place for photographs."

"Answer him, then."

The Russian took back the radio and turned the pointer to *transmit*. "Hello, Waverly," he said, his mouth close to the microphone grille, "this is Kuryakin. Hello, Waverly – come in, please. . . . Hello, Waverly . . ."

He turned the pointer back to *receive*. But only the bleeping continued. No voice answered from the tiny speaker – which was not surprising, as he had kept his thumb firmly on a small button at the side of the casing. Unless the button was released, the radio would not transmit.

"Try again," Ononu ordered.

Illya repeated the charade. And again the high-pitched pips provided his only reply. After a time they ceased.

"It must have gone wrong," Kuryakin said, shaking the set vaguely.

"I will take charge of it," the Colonel said, holding out his hand.

"But it will be of no use to you. It cannot be tuned to different wave-lengths: you can only use it in conjunction with similar sets which have been synchronized with it. It is useless by itself."

"Radios are always useful in guerilla warfare."

"But I tell you it is useless to you. Besides, it is broken."

"Then you will not be inconvenienced by the lack of it."

Ononu took the receiver and put it in his own pocket. "I have decided," he said. "I have decided to permit you to proceed and seek your friend – but only because of what you told me earlier: that you had received General Mazzari's personal accord. This will be checked – and I must warn you that, if it should prove to be untrue, you will regret it."

"It is true."

"Good. Then, apart from one small formality, I need not detain you further. As underground forces, you understand, we must not remain too long in the same place. More normally, we keep to the mountains – however, the day is at hand. The Nya Nyerere will soon be marching openly, the acknowledged force for law and order in the land."

"And the formality?"

"We must search your effects, lest there might be something dangerous to us – or of use to us."

Illya shrugged angrily and gestured towards the Landrover. He stood fuming in the searing sunlight, sweat plastering his hair to his forehead, as the soldiers expertly unrolled his baggage and handed up the contents for Ononu's examination.

The mercurial Colonel "requisitioned" – as Kuryakin had feared – the collapsible U.N.C.L.E. gun and its ammunition. He also took a parcel of miniature grenades, a bundle of phosphorus lock-destroyers, a rifle with a telescopic sight, and a pair of homing devices in a case, similar to those used by Solo. "You appear, Mr Kuryakin, to anticipate some hostile reaction from your subjects," he said drily.

"The area is far from any human habitation and practically unexplored, as I said. One has to prepare for anything."

"You will be able to move the better without the excess weight – for you will be unable to take your car the whole way, you know. It is a rare thing to see a vehicle at all in these parts. ... Which being so, we will relieve you of one of these also." He motioned a man to take out one of a pair of 14-gallon jerricans filled with petrol which were housed against the flat back of the Landrover.

"But I shall not be able to replace them," Illya expostulated. "The tank needs replenishing now – and I have perhaps two hundred miles to go. Plus at least another four hundred before I find a petrol station on the return journey . . ."

"As I said, you will not be able to take your vehicle the whole way to the forest," Ononu remarked smoothly. "The scarcity of gasolene now will ensure that you do not stray into regions where you have no business, in your attempts to find alternative routes. Besides, you have the pleasure of knowing that you are advancing the Cause."

Kuryakin raised his arms and let them drop helplessly by his sides. There was no point in arguing: there was nothing he could do; and if he provoked Ononu too much, the soldier was quite capable of taking the whole car and abandoning him in the wilderness. At least they had left him his field glasses and his three cameras – one of which was a dummy and fired eight .32 bullets in rapid succession from what appeared to be a rangefinder. In his trouser pocket, too, was the cigarette-lighter pistol, with its sleep darts.

After driving two and a quarter hours, he reached the fork where the roads for Wau and Halakaz diverged. There had once been a settlement at the junction, but all that remained now was the familiar patch of blackened and seared ground, pock-marked with jagged stumps of walls. From a horizontal branch jutting out over the road, a scorched tree dangled the bodies of five hanged men – naked, decomposing, the eyes plucked out by vultures. Illya shuddered and swung the Landrover around the grisly spectacle to take the right hand track towards Halakaz

The scrub had given place to a mean variety of bushes and squat trees as the road mounted. Now the trees thickened and the angle of incline grew more steep. Soon the Landrover was labouring in bottom gear up what appeared to be a channel carved in the solid bedrock.

After several miles of this, the trail flattened out – although it grew no smoother – and Illya saw that they were crossing a plateau of bare volcanic rock surrounded on all sides by steep, sugar-loaf hills covered in dense vegetation. The foliage was brownish-grey in colour and could under no stretch of the imagination be termed rich; but it was a welcome change from the eternal monotony of the thorn tree desert. At least there must be some water about somewhere. . . .

The Landrover had plunged into several valleys and climbed the steep slopes on the far side before Illya saw any, however. Then suddenly the trail, instead of ascending after it had crossed a dry river bed, turned and followed the watercourse along a twisting defile which opened out into a wide, shallow valley four or five miles across. And in the middle of the valley a trickle of brown water flowed sluggishly in a deep *wadi*. Birds flapped into the air and a herd of deer-like creatures – there must have been several hundred of them – galloped off in a cloud of dust as the vehicle approached. They were the first living creatures Illya had seen since he left Colonel Ononu and his detachment that morning.

He stopped the car at the bottom of the *wadi*, replenished his radiator with some of the brackish water, and poured petrol from his remaining jerrican into the tank. Then, after eating some cold food from his pack, he drove on towards the hills on the far side of the valley.

The topography was different here – the slopes gentler, the vegetation lusher and more verdant. To balance this advantage was the fact that, among the undergrowth, the trail was at times very difficult to find. Several times he had to stop, get out, and cast around for some time before he could identify the route.

Towards the end of the afternoon, he found himself emerging from an area of dense forest into a small glade floored with plants which had bright violet flowers. The trail vanished among the trees on the far side of the open space. But across the middle, a chasm barred the way.

Illya pulled up and walked to the edge of the fissure. Some gigantic upheaval aeons ago had split the earth open as though it had been cleft with a vast axe. On either side, the trees closed in and lined the gorge as far as he could see. Far below, a thread of water glistened in the shadows – and among the smooth rocks he could make out the splintered remnants of what had been a plank bridge. The sheer faces of the cleft overhung at the top and the gap was no more than four or five feet where the bridge had been; a child of ten could have leaped it with ease. But for the Landrover it was an impassable barrier. . . .

For minutes, the Russian pondered. To go back was hopeless: he had no means of knowing how far round he would have to go. And in any case no alternative route was marked on the map. Equally, without the right kind of tools and tackle, it would be impossible to fell trees and fashion some kind of makeshift bridge. There was nothing else for it: he must abandon the vehicle and continue on foot.

Once more he consulted the map. So far as he could make out from the undetailed markings, he was still more than thirty miles short of Halakaz. He would have to sleep somewhere in the jungle and walk there tomorrow. It was an awkward predicament; it could be dangerous. On the other hand it could have been much worse. Perhaps he would be able to hire a mule or a camel in the town.

He backed the Landrover into the trees and bumped a hundred yards off the track among the undergrowth. It was quite invisible from the trail and there was just a chance it might remain undetected. Making a compact roll of his sleeping bag, a couple of sweaters and the remainder of his provisions, he slung field glasses, Hasselblad and the gun-camera over his shoulder and returned to the chasm. After pitching the roll across, he retreated a few paces, ran up and jumped lightly over the gap.

The trail twisted and turned among the giant trees. The undergrowth was now positively luxuriant and long strands of creeper hung down from branches far above his head. It was airless and sombre, the atmosphere moist and humming with invisible insects; but from what he could see of the sky through the treetops, he estimated that there was still an hour or more of daylight. He must press on as far as he could.

For half an hour he trudged through the forest. And then, to his astonishment, he heard voices. Cautiously rounding a thicket, he found himself face to face with a woman in riding breeches carrying an elephant gun.

At first he was irresistibly reminded of General Mazzari, for her accoutrements gleamed from the tips of her knee-length leather boots to the lenses of the sunglasses masking her eyes. But there the resemblance ended. Although deeply bronzed, she was a white woman, small-waisted, about thirty-five years old, and wearing, of all things, a Sam Browne belt. She wore lipstick and her ash-blonde hair was absurdly gathered on the nape of her neck in a black velvet bow.

"And from where have *you* suddenly sprung, young man?" she enquired in English. Her voice was deep, husky, overlaid with a trace of accent – Swiss, perhaps? – that he could not quite place.

Illya dropped the roll at his feet with a sigh of relief and told her about the chasm.

"Yes, the arabs destroyed the bridge six months ago," she said. "I suppose they thought it might hinder the Nya Nyerere. But there are dozens of places further down where they can cross. However, that doesn't help you. You had better stay with us tonight and tell me all about it while we eat."

She led the way back to a clearing where a fair-sized encampment was laid out. Two orderly lines of fly-sheeted tents faced a charcoal fire from which drifted an agreeable smell of cooking. At one side, bales and crates of stores were neatly stacked. Among them, Illya saw, was a theodolite on a tripod. There seemed to be about a dozen Negro bearers in the camp, and at least three white men.

The woman's name, she told him, was Rosa Harsch. She was a geomorphologist, surveying and mapping the great triangle of uncharted forest which lay between Halakaz, Wau and Wadi Elmira on behalf of a development corporation – which she did not name. "There's thousands of square miles of jungle here practically unexplored," she said. "Underneath, most of it's limestone – but the strata are stiff with unconformities and there are igneous intrusions all over the place and probably veins of anything you care to mention. It is a most interesting area."

"It seems surprisingly poorly provided with rivers, when you consider how rich the vegetation is," Illya said.

"Ah, that is because they all run underground: the limestone is riddled with potholes and caves and subterranean channels, like the Department of Haute Savoie in France. Most of them drain into the Bahr-el-Arab, the Bahr-el-Homr or the Soueh – and thus eventually into the Bahr-el-Ghaza river."

While they ate a surprisingly sophisticated meal, Illya extended the story of his photographic expedition, mentioning the fictitious Waverly he was supposed to meet. He was getting increasingly anxious about being out of touch with Solo and wondered if perhaps Rosa Harsch might have come across him.

"No, we have seen nobody except refugees from the burned villages," she said. "And the forest is full of them. Trying not to starve, poor devils, and wondering all the time what is going to happen to them.... So far as hiring animals at Halakaz is concerned, forget it. Halakaz is a six-hundred-year-old mud fort with one street of tumbledown hovels leading up to it. If the inhabitants had seen a spare beast in the past ten years they would have cooked and eaten it.... Where is the actual place of the rendezvous with your partner?"

"It was supposed to be somewhere near Gabotomi – only we were to keep in touch by radio, and mine was taken from me by an irregular Colonel named Ononu. ... Talking of

Gabotomi, I believe that is a most interesting place, although it is not on the map. These so-called forbidden cities often are. Perhaps you could give me more explicit directions how to find it?"

But Rosa Harsch, whose replies had until then been detailed and specific, suddenly appeared to succumb to an attack of vagueness. She wasn't quite sure, she said, where the place was – if it existed at all – and so far as she knew they had been nowhere near it. A few minutes later she rose to her feet and clapped her hands. "If you will excuse me," she said, "there are two matters of a disciplinary nature which must be attended to before we retire. . . . Mustapha! Ibrahim! Prepare things for the punishments, please."

Two tall Nubians, who seemed to be in charge of the bearers, started shouting orders and the camp suddenly buzzed with activity. A trestle table was set up in the firelight and a bearer wearing only a pair of shorts was led up to it. He leaned forward over the end of the table. The Nubians spread his legs and tied the ankles to the table legs, binding his wrists and attaching them with another rope to the far trestle, so that he was stretched forward across the length of the table.

The woman walked into her tent and reappeared with a peeled switch. "This man was discovered helping himself to more than his share of the liquor ration," she said unemotionally. "Six strokes."

She approached the table, measured her distance, and raised her arm. The switch hissed down and raised a livid weal on the victim's body. Illya watched in astonishment as the following five strokes fell in metronomic precision on the same spot. Apart from a sharp intake of breath at each blow, the pinioned man uttered no sound. Nor was there any comment from the rest of the party, who watched in a grave-faced circle around the fire. As soon as the last stroke had fallen, Rosa Harsch turned her back and the Nubians rapidly released the man, who limped back to his tent. A minute later they led a thin, bearded white man of about twenty-six to the table.

"This man, by his carelessness in his duties as clerk, caused us to lose a rucksack containing notebooks filled with irreplaceable data," Rosa Harsch said. "Ten strokes." And the process was repeated exactly as before.

When it was over, the members of the party dispersed to their various sleeping quarters and the woman returned to Illya by the fire. The flickering light smoothed out the network of fine wrinkles around her eyes and softened the contours of her face. From a certain rigidity about the waist and the twin bulges of flesh at each side of her back just below the arms, he guessed that she was wearing a laced corset beneath the shirt. But for all that she was still remarkably attractive.

"I see you have no colour bar in your expedition," he said lightly, as she unbuckled the Sam Browne and dropped to the ground beside him.

"No," she said seriously. "No colour bar. Everybody is treated the same. It is best. In places as remote and as dangerous as this, it is unfortunately necessary to impose strict discipline. Without it, they take advantage – all of them. And that impairs efficiency. Without complete efficiency, an expedition of this sort is doomed from the start."

"They all seem to take it for granted. Nobody resents such . . . discipline . . . being administered by a woman?"

"But of course not. I am the leader of the expedition."

She offered Kuryakin a cigarette, lit one herself. "And now," she said, leaning towards him in the glow of the embers, "it is time to relax. Tell me about yourself: you could interest me, young man . . ."

CHAPTER TWELVE

SCHOOL IS DISMISSED . . .

WHILE Illya had been filling his radiator from the trickle of water in the *wadi*, Napoleon Solo, more than a hundred and fifty miles to the northeast, was guiding his horse between the stones of a moraine which sloped gradually down to a plain. Somewhere ahead of him, the caravan with the camel carrying the container of Uranium 235 was winding its way among the tall grasses and scrub oak that had supplanted the ubiquitous thorn trees.

He rode slowly, the homing device open on the saddle in front of him. At first, turning the pointer to ensure that he was taking the direction in which the bleeps were loudest was almost a formality: the trail was well marked and there was no other route the caravan could have taken. Later in the afternoon, when he was climbing another of the interminable series of limestone ridges with which the country was barred, he had cause to be glad of his foresight; for the track itself petered out among a wilderness of rock outcrops, and he was constantly obliged to check and recheck his route.

Such food as he had, had been abandoned with the camel and he was ravenously hungry. He was anxious about the horse, too, for the animal had taken neither food nor water since he had escaped from Ahmed and the soldiers.

He had ripped a length of cloth from his burnous to improvise a head-dress against the scorching rays of the sun. The remainder of his robes he had discarded and buried with the "pilgrim's" papers. Now – thankful that he had been wearing his bush shirt and shorts underneath them – he was again beardless, his nose normal, in the guise of Napoleon Solo, mineralogist of Russian extraction, equipped with a *laissez-passer* countersigned by His Excellency Hassan Hamid. . . .

Several times he attempted to contact Illya, but the radio remained obstinately silent.

From the top of the ridge, he swept the country beyond

with his glasses. It was definitely becoming less barren; there were squares of cultivation here and there, and vegetation covered the rolling contours more thickly. Far off towards a range of tree-covered hills which reared, blue-hazed, against the horizon, a long line of dust marked the position of the caravan. He slid the binoculars back into their case and rode on down.

Twice he had to skirt villages – no longer the mud-walled arab variety, but circles of huts in the African manner – but he saw nobody. Once, though, he fancied he heard the sound of distant rifle fire.

He was within a mile of the wooded hills when he saw a column of smoke rising above the trees off to the right. A moment later, hooves thundered on hard ground and he trotted the horse out of sight behind a maize hedge just before a squadron of arab cavalry thundered past in a cloud of dust. There were about thirty of them, shouting and laughing and waving their rifles above their heads as they rode. Two of them carried the bound figures of African women across their saddles; a third dragged behind his horse on a length of rope the lacerated body of a man.

Solo waited in his place of concealment until the dust had settled. He switched on the homer again: the pips were still sounding loud and clear. He could afford the time to investigate.

Walking the horse warily between the trees, he advanced towards the column of smoke.

When he was about two hundred yards away, he found a patch of grass where the horse could graze. Tethering the animal to a sapling, he drew the Mauser and went forward on foot.

The village was completely concealed in a shallow depression. As he trod down the slope, Solo's nostrils were assailed by the bitter stench of burning and death. Most of the inhabitants must have fled, but there were a dozen bodies sprawled in the dusty space enclosed by the ring of gutted huts.

The flames had died down, but half a dozen of the burned huts still spiralled smoke into the air. The only thing standing was the stone-built end wall of a building rather larger than the others.

Solo walked around the corner of the wall – and stopped in astonishment. The rest of the building had been made of wood, and all that remained of it was a tangle of charred embers from which wisps of smoke still rose. But it had obviously been some kind of school. Hardwood desks with iron frames had escaped the conflagration and still stood upright among the debris. What was oddest of all was the size of the desks: with their attached seats, they were big enough for full-grown adults!

The agent turned to look at the end wall. A scorched teacher's desk had fallen forward among the blackened timbers of a dias. Behind it, a blackboard was still attached to the plaster. Glancing idly at the chalked figures, he drew in his breath with a gasp of surprise. The top line read: *Réaction de chaine: fission de l'Uranium*. And beneath this was a diagram.

At the foot of the board was written:

W (énergie de la transmutation) = mc²
(c = vit. de la lumière d'après l'équivalence de la masse et de l'énergie)
L'Uranium . . .

"My God!" Solo exclaimed aloud. "Atomic physics *here*! They must be running a school for future warmongers. . . . It seems I'm getting warm, after all!"

Hurrying back to the horse, he noticed a scrap of white paper lying under the trees. He found that it was a sheet from a loose-leaf notebook, on which was written:

La Famille du Radium
Uranium $^{238}_{92}$ $\longrightarrow$ $xT5$ $\longrightarrow$ *Radium* $^{226}_{88}$, *en radon* $^{222}_{84}$
ou emanation $\longrightarrow$ $xT7$ $\longrightarrow$ *Polonium* $^{210}_{84}$ $\longrightarrow$ *Plomb*
$^{206}_{82}$ *(stable).*

Neutrons (en mitraille du Béryllium + des Hélions)
Azote $^{14}_{7}$ + *Neutron* $^{1}_{0}$ $\longrightarrow$ *Bore* $^{11}_{5}$ + *Hélion* $^{4}_{2}$

"Well, at least some of the class seem to have got away," Solo muttered as he remounted and rode off along the trail.

It looked as though, wherever THRUSH were conveying the Uranium 235, they must be organizing courses of instruction in its use among the dissident Africans. Whether the sack of the village by the arabs had anything to do with this, or whether it was merely a coincidence, he had at present no means of knowing. In any case, it seemed reasonable that the destination of the lead canister might be near at hand.

A few miles farther on among the wooded hills, he reined in the horse on a crest and took out his glasses. Three ridges away, he could clearly spot the caravan traversing an open space among the trees. The powerful Zeiss lenses showed him the striped blanket still in position on the camel he was following.

He rode on down the track, now clearly marked and in greater use than most of the route over which he had travelled.

He was within sight of the open space where he had seen the caravan when he suddenly noticed that the bleeps on the homer were growing fainter. Puzzled, he stopped. He knew the train had come this way because he had watched it; and he knew, furthermore, that the camel had still been with it then. They couldn't possibly have accelerated and got so far ahead that they were out of range. Why should the signal have lost strength if he was – as he knew – on the right track? He rode on farther – and the bleeps grew fainter still.

Had the beast carrying the canister broken away from the main body? He halted again and swung the homer questioningly round. There was no sign of the signal strengthening in any direction tangential to the trail. It was only when he wheeled completely about that he realized the answer.

The bleeps increased in volume when he was facing back the way he had come.

Although the camel was still with the caravan, the canister – or at least the homing device he had placed with it – had been left somewhere along the route. Solo cantered back along the track, his pulses quickening with the thought of action at last.

It was a simple matter to follow the signals. They grew

100

stronger and stronger as he went along. It looked as though the canister was now stationary. . . .

The homer finally led him off the track and in among the woods. When the signals were registering their maximum, he dismounted, drew the Mauser, and tiptoed cautiously through the undergrowth as the device directed him. There was a puzzled frown on his face: he must be almost there – yet there were no signs of the buildings or installations he had expected. At length he came to a small clearing with a sandy pit in the middle.

In the centre of the pit was the lead canister. It was open, Solo saw with a momentary thrill of alarm . . . but the narrow core in the heart of the lead shield was empty.

Except for the homer placed neatly in the middle of it.

The agent's scalp prickled. There was something all wrong about this: the deserted glade, the canister conveniently displayed in the centre of the pit, the absence of buildings . . . it was too much like a stage setting, a set-up.

"You had better drop the pistol. There are automatic rifles covering you from all around," a voice said quietly in arabic.

Solo whirled. Among the tree trunks enclosing the glade, a ring of soldiers with rifles at the hip stood in the shadows. He pitched the Mauser away from him and stood waiting.

A squat, powerfully-built African wearing a French paratroop beret and the insignia of a Colonel on the shoulderstraps of his bush shirt stepped forward and picked the gun up.

"We thought you would turn up to collect your little toy," he said affably. "What kept you so long? We have been waiting for you. . . ."

CHAPTER THIRTEEN

A SURPRISE FOR ILLYA

ILLYA KURYAKIN marched the whole of the next day with Rosa Harsch and her retinue. He was in an awkward predicament, for the woman herself continued to be deliberately evasive about her destination, and he could not decide at what point he should break away and head off on his own. Since, for the moment, the expedition appeared to be following the route he would himself have chosen, he stayed with them.

The forest grew denser and steamier. The hills became higher. And when again they stopped to make camp for the night, he estimated that they must be on a level with Halakaz though about twenty miles to the east.

While the enigmatic Miss Harsch was issuing instructions on the siting of tents to Mustapha, the young bearded man who had been beaten the previous evening manoeuvred himself close to Kuryakin. "I don't know who you are," he said. "But if you are trying to make your way to Gabotomi, it lies no more than ten or twelve miles due northeast of here."

"I don't know who *you* are," the Russian replied, "but thank you. The information will be of great use to me. Do you know the place yourself?"

"We have been ... near there. We have looked down upon it. But it is necessary to proceed with extreme caution: the town – it was originally only a settlement – is tucked away at the bottom of a steep gorge. It is impossible to descend the cliffs at either side and behind it. The only entrance is along a steep valley leading directly to the gate – and that is too well guarded to force. The place is the headquarters of the Nya Nyerere. There are hundreds of their soldiers there, and there seem to be assault courses, training grounds, lecture theatres – the full equipment of a military academy."

"I don't know why you should tell me all this – "

"It is necessary to make a stand against autocracy at

102

times," the young man said vaguely. He had a thick central European accent.

"Ah. The – er – punishments? I confess that I was surprised to find you made no protests."

"Orders. Besides, it was part of the deal when we signed on; it was made clear that infringements would be punished and we agreed to accept those punishments if they were merited – all of us. Also the money is very good. . . . Nevertheless, one's self-respect demands a gesture from time to time. . . . I must go: it would not do for me to be seen talking to you for too long." And he glided unobtrusively away.

Illya took his leave as soon as they struck camp the following morning, telling Rosa Harsch that he expected to find his partner some way east or southeast of their present position.

She took his hand in a firm grip as they said their farewells – and seemed reluctant to let it go. "I wish you luck, my friend," she said huskily, "and I ask you to take care. If you have need of help, come back to us: we shall be taking readings for several days about twenty miles north of here. . . . Anyway, I have a feeling that we shall meet again, you and I."

She stared full into his eyes for a moment and then, abruptly releasing his hand, turned and creaked off down the trail after her bearers, the switch of blonde hair with its black bow bouncing up and down on her muscular shoulders.

Kuryakin made his way due east for about half a mile along a side trail, in case he was being watched, and then plunged into the forest in the direction indicated by the young man with the beard. Half an hour's hard going brought him to another narrow track running roughly the right way, and for the next two hours, he made good time. By noon, he was wedged into a tree fork, binoculars to his eyes, looking down on the rooftops of Gabotomi from a ridge above and behind the ravine in which the place was built.

It certainly did look like an army camp. Between the geometrically arranged buildings – constructed, astonishingly, of red brick in the European style – there was a constant coming and going of squads of men, most of them Negroes and all of them in uniform. He could distinguish a parade ground with platoons at their drill, a carefully laid out battle course, and several groups seated cross-legged on the ground who were listening to open-air lectures complete with blackboards and lantern slides. From far below, the crackle of rifle fire drifted up from a line of butts just outside the settlement.

If – as seemed probable from the hints dropped by Mazzari and Ononu – the Nya Nyerere was in some way being aided by THRUSH, this was obviously the place where it was being done. But why? What was in it for THRUSH? How could the overthrow of the Sudanese government in the north aid the evil organization's plans for world conquest?

Illya's biggest surprise was still to come, however. And it was not until he turned his back on Gabotomi that he received it. He had manoeuvred himself round in the tree fork and was sweeping the scores of miles of wooded hills to the east with his glasses when suddenly he gave an exclamation of amazement. For a moment, he had thought . . . Yes! There it was again! In the magnified circle of terrain revealed by the lenses ran a section of modern, metalled highway. . . .

He lowered the binoculars and rubbed his eyes. The road was still there. Now he knew where to look, he could see it with the naked eye: a broad carriageway running along an open crest a couple of miles away, to link up with an undulating concrete swathe that could only be a landing strip!

As he watched, a vehicle came in sight. It was travelling quite fast – a squareish blue utility car, probably a Renault 4L, he thought. He followed its course along the road until it disappeared from sight behind a belt of trees. Idly, estimating its speed, he traced its invisible path behind the wood and waited for it to emerge on the far side. Promptly, as he had anticipated, the 4L reappeared and continued along the macadam at the same velocity.

Only now it was red.

For the second time, the Russian rubbed his eyes. What kind of conjuring trick was this? A blue car, travelling at about forty miles per hour, disappeared momentarily behind a line of trees – to re-emerge at exactly the same speed, at exactly the right time, in a different colour! There was no other traffic on the road; the wood wasn't long enough for there to have been a substitution – and in any case there wouldn't be room for a second car to get up that speed before it was clear of the trees. . . .

It reminded him irresistibly of a relay race where a baton is handed from one runner to the next. Only in this case there had been neither the room nor the time for such a takeover. He felt he must at once find out the secret of the car that changed colour!

He slid to the ground and set off as quickly as he could in the direction of the roadway. It took him over an hour and a half to traverse the two intervening valleys. The undergrowth was dense, and he had to be especially careful, for there was what appeared to be a fully manned garrison in the neighbourhood. Despite the proximity of Gabotomi, however, he saw nobody on the way and finally emerged from a thicket to find himself at the edge of the road.

The carriageway had been laid about six months, he judged: a twenty-foot strip of blacktop running from an airstrip in the middle of uncharted, unexplored country to . . . where? The runway was innocent of buildings: there was not so much as a hut in sight. Beyond it, the forest closed in again – and to the other side, the road curved out of sight towards the belt of trees where the metamorphosis of the 4L had occurred. Keeping well hidden by the bushes fringeing the road, he walked cautiously towards the wood. And, like most conjuring tricks, the explanation was simple once you knew how it was done.

There had in fact been two different vehicles – and the visual illusion had been possible because there were also two different roads!

Behind the trees, the road he was following dipped suddenly to run into a tunnel leading underground. And, just beyond, was the exit from a second tunnel, slightly to one side, carrying another highway on into the distance. The arrangement was similar to the underpasses carrying ring roads around modern cities – and it had just happened that, while he watched, a car had emerged from the exit tunnel coincidentally with another, travelling at the same speed, plunging into the entrance . . .

Dropping to the ground, he wormed his way through the

undergrowth until he could train his glasses uninterruptedly on the tunnel mouth.

It was arched, tall enough to take the largest army truck, and well engineered in limestone blocks. The stonework continued out along the sides of the sunken road until it had risen to ground level. Inside the entrance, a row of electric bulbs in the tunnel roof parallelled the sweep of the roadway as it turned steeply aside and spiralled underground. The other tunnel, from which the red car had emerged, no doubt performed the same manoeuvre in the opposite direction – and the two roads would presumably meet at some common point below. But what kind of subterranean enclave was served by these routes?

Illya crawled farther along, so that he could see a greater distance inside the curving tunnel. Just around the first bend, the sandbags and slits of a redoubt broke the even surface of the wall. So the direct entry, as he had imagined, was out of the question. . . .

Although the sun was nearing its zenith and the heat was becoming insupportable, he decided that he must prospect further without delay. In the absence of radio contact with Solo, the only thing he could do was to continue on his own. He began to work his way back to the landing strip through the woods on the far side of the road. When he was perhaps half way there, he pushed through a tangle of bushes and froze suddenly into silence. The ground opened beneath his feet. Hidden in the undergrowth, the mouth of a concrete-walled shaft yawned before him.

He peered over the lip. In the shadowed depths of the shaft, the slim, tapering nose of a missile gleamed wickedly.

Kuryakin gave a low whistle of astonishment. It looked as though the confidence of the Nya Nyerere was well founded – and it looked, also, as if the destination of the stolen Uranium isotopes was inextricably bound up with the puzzling alliance of THRUSH and a band of nationalist guerillas. . . .

During the next half hour, he found three more underground silos of the same pattern, each with its missile in place. Heaven knew what ramifications were to be found somewhere below his feet!

Before he reached the airstrip, his attention was diverted by a persistent, low roaring noise which had for some time been forcing its way into his consciousness. He glanced up. Over the trees away to his left a haze hung in the air, half way between a mist and a thin smoke. It was too hot now, anyway, to venture out into the full glare of the sun by the runway. He decided to investigate.

The noise increased in volume as he approached. The undergrowth became denser and more luxuriant. The mist resolved itself into a cloud of fine spray hanging over a waterfall.

But the breadth and scale of the thing surprised Illya yet again. The river was wider than he would have expected, shallow and fast moving. It flowed across a plain whose existence he had not suspected, divided around a number of small islands on the lip of the falls, and then twisted away down a narrow gorge – presumably to vanish underground and reappear in the valley in which Gabotomi was situated. The falls themselves were staggering: a semicircle of separate cascades which poured over a fifty-foot ledge from between the islands, coalesced in a turbulent pool, and then leaped in a single drop over a sheer cliff fully a hundred and fifty feet high.

For some minutes, Kuryakin remained fascinated by the grandeur of the scene, his senses battered into quiescence by the volume of sound. Then, as his mind automatically began accepting and rejecting and sifting the evidence offered to his eyes and ears, he noticed a discrepancy: surely the flow of water running away from the foot of the waterfall was appreciably – most markedly – less than that arriving at the top?

The more he looked, the more obvious it became. Perhaps this was one of the places mentioned by Rosa Harsch, where the greater part of the river vanished underground, to continue by a subterranean channel in the limestone. He scanned the falls, searching for some trace of the sink-hole. It must be somewhere in the seething pool between the cascades and the final, single fall over the cliff. . . .

Yes: there were signs of dark openings in the hollowed-out rock behind several of the initial falls – and there was something else, too: unmistakably, he could see patches of concrete among the glistening rock. . . . Somewhere behind those deafening cascades, man had been improving on the works of nature.

Concealing the Hasselblad and his field glasses in a clump of bushes, he slung the waterproof gun-camera around his neck and scrambled down a narrow path zigzagging the steep bank towards the pool.

In two minutes, he was drenched to the skin. But after the heat of the day, the dank, ferny atmosphere of the ravine and the moisture of the spume were as refreshing as a cool drink. Slipping and sliding on the wet moss covering the rocks, he reached the level of the basin.

The water was boiling – shading from an absinthe green near the foaming impact of the falls to a deep violet in the centre of the pool. And once he approached, he could see at once that his reasoning was correct. The water spilling over the lip and falling a hundred and fifty feet to the gorge below was nothing more than an overflow; by the far greater part swirled back from the bottom of the pool to go roaring down a series of conduits slanting into the rock behind the cascades.

As he had expected, the falls had hollowed out an overhang in the cliff and it was possible to walk along a rock shelf behind the curtain of falling water and the face. Treading with infinite care, he edged along the slimy rock behind the first cascade, slithered across an open space, and went in behind the second.

Here were two of the conduits – giant ferro-concrete tubes ducting the water into the bowels of the earth at an angle of sixty degrees. Crossing the deep channels leading the torrents from pool to conduit were small arched bridges with single guard rails.

Behind the third waterfall, Illya found three conduits, similarly linked by concrete bridges – only here the centre one was larger: a vaulted tunnel with the water thundering down a course laid in its floor. At the far end of the passage, perhaps seventy feet below, he could see light, the curved corners of huge turbines, the bases of generators. He had obviously stumbled on a vast underground power station – the source, no doubt, of the electricity lighting the road tunnels he had seen.

Soaked as he was, he shivered in the chill, moist semi-darkness behind the cascade. He never knew what it was that made him look up at that moment – certainly no sound could have penetrated his mind over the roar of the falls. But he did look up . . . up and out over the stretch of rock separating the third and fourth cascades.

They were farther apart than the others, these two, and a guard rail snaked across the undulations of wet rock between them. Leaning nonchalantly against it, a soldier was in the act of raising his rifle to fire at the Russian from a distance of about thirty feet.

Almost in a reflex action, Kuryakin whipped the gun-camera to his eye and pressed the release. The man's dark face split open in an O of astonishment. The rifle dropped from his hands and slithered down the rock into the water. For a moment, he teetered against the rail . . . and then slowly slumped back over it and fell into the pool. His body sank at once, to reappear bobbing like a cork far out in the middle of the maelstrom.

The agent expected it to be sucked towards the conduits, but after a while some undercurrent tugged it towards the side of the pool, where it caught momentarily on a branch, freed itself, spun slowly in an eddy, and then began to move – remorselessly and with increasing speed – towards the lip and the hundred and fifty foot drop beyond. For ten seconds, he lost sight of it again . . . but the dead man made a final horrifying appearance, rearing grotesquely up from the water on the very brink of the chasm before he plunged from sight.

It would be a long time before his body was discovered, but his absence could be noticed at any moment. Illya decided that it was time he went.

After he had recovered his camera and glasses, he resumed his route through the forest to the airstrip. It presented a different aspect now, he saw when he gained the fringe of the trees. While he had been out of earshot of the falls, a plane had landed: a twin-fuselage transport whose cargo a squad of soldiers were unloading into a convoy of trucks drawn up on the concrete.

With his wet clothes steaming in the sun, the agent lay

beneath a bush and watched them through his glasses. Most of the cargo was crated – and judging from the way in which it was handled, the machinery inside was delicate.

Half an hour later, the transhipment was completed. The aircraft trundled to the far end of the runway, turned, and took off. The convoy had formed up and was heading back towards the road and the tunnel before the drone of its twin engines had died away over the forest.

The trucks passed quite close to Illya's hiding place. There were eight of them – 14-cwt vehicles with canvas tops painted in drab camouflage – but, so far as he could see, only the first three carried guards, who stood on the footboards at each side of the driver's cabin.

On impulse, he rose to his feet and ran through the long grass to intercept them. He reached the road just as the last truck slowed to make the turn from the landing strip, paused until it was past him, and then emerged on to the macadam. In three quick strides he was level with the tailboard. As the truck accelerated, he grasped the hinged panel, pushed aside the canvas flap and hauled himself up and over into the interior.

Two big crates filled most of the space inside – stoutly built containers of one-inch planking with reinforcing battens on all sides. He saw no contents specifications or delivery instructions stencilled on the wood.

He was relieved to see that, apart from the crates, the back of the truck was empty – nor was there any window between it and the driver's cabin. Panting a little after his exertion, he settled down to wait. He had no fixed idea of what he was going to do when the truck stopped. He was tired of inactivity and it seemed one way of getting past the guards at the tunnel mouth. It was unlikely that they would search their own vehicles after so short a journey; he must just hope that he would have an opportunity to slip out unnoticed before the cargo was unloaded.

They had been going for perhaps a minute and a half when he heard voices shouting on the road outside. Cautiously, he peered through the crack between the flap and the body of the truck. They were passing a file of soldiers marching in the same direction, and the driver and his mate were exchanging pleasantries with the men on foot.

In the middle of the file, Illya saw, two soldiers marched about ten feet apart carrying between them a long pole which was balanced on their shoulders.

And slung under it like a sloth, with the pole passing between his bound wrists and ankles, was the unconscious figure of Napoleon Solo. . . .

A moment later the truck began to sink below ground level as the road dipped between the stone walls which led to the tunnel mouth. Kuryakin drew back behind one of the crates. There was nothing he could do for Solo at this moment. He could not see whether the marching men were following the convoy into the tunnel or going on somewhere else – perhaps to Gabotomi. In any event, he could best help by getting inside the THRUSH fortress undetected and working from there.

They appeared to have driven straight past the guards. For some minutes the truck continued to descend in a series of tight curves, then the road flattened out and they went straight ahead for what seemed about a quarter of a mile. Finally, the vehicle made a tight right turn, stopped, reversed, came forward on right-hand lock and stopped again.

The first impression Illya had when the engine was switched off was of echos: the boots of the soldiers as they climbed down from the trucks, a distant hammering, the pervasive hum of machinery, a confusion of voices calling – all these blurred and repeated themselves in a great swell of noise.

He inched forward and again put his eye to the crack between tailboard and flap. They were drawn up with the other seven trucks in a bay off an immense cavern in the rock. Both the roof and the farther reaches of the huge chamber were lost in shadows. Nearer at hand, arc lights blazed on an army of workmen who were erecting some complicated apparatus from a scaffold. Beyond a stack of crates similar to those in the truck, an arch in the natural limestone led to another cavern even bigger. In the bright light which shone through, he could see dreamlike figures in asbestos suits and protective helmets with perspex eyepieces busy about the spirals of great cooling tubes. To one side, a section of a gigantic silver sphere that could only be an atomic reactor bulged into view. He need look no further for the destination of the stolen Uranium 235. . . .

The convoy drivers, their mates and the escorting guards were all grouped around an officer issuing instructions some way off, their backs towards the bay. Now was his chance. Lifting the flap as little as possible, he dropped to the ground and slid around to the front of the truck. Crouched between the radiator and the rock wall, out of sight of the soldiers, he looked around him for a place to hide.

A little way to his left, hidden from the men in the cavern by another truck, a doorway opened into the wall. He edged along to it, listened, turned the handle, and slipped through.

He found himself in a long passage with closed doors on either side. Electric bulbs glowed in the roof. At the far end, an opening led to the dark reaches of another cave. The humming noise was louder now: he must be approaching the generating station he had seen from behind the cascades.

Kuryakin flitted silently along the corridor and into the cave. It was empty and unlit – but through it was yet another chamber, in whose dim lighting he could make out the squat shapes of transformers.

He hesitated. Should he conceal himself in this empty cavern? – or should he return to the scene of activity and try to hide somewhere there? . . . Perhaps the latter – then he could emerge and investigate further when work had stopped for the day. . . .

He turned. In the lighted entrance to the passage, General Mazzari was standing, a heavy Walther automatic in his hand.

"Not many white rhino down here," he said mildly. "I think you and I had better have a little talk, old chap. . . ."

CHAPTER FOURTEEN

INSIDE THE UNDERGROUND FORTRESS

GANGS of men armed with pneumatic picks were trying to drill off the top of Napoleon Solo's head before it exploded. They were too late: the world spun away in fragments, leaving a swirling red haze through which the face of the foreman peered at him apologetically.

". . . necessary to hit you quite so hard," the foreman was saying; "but in any case the journey here would probably have caused you more hardship than the blow and its after effects."

Solo's eyes were half open. The foreman's face sharpened in focus and a room gradually assembled itself behind him. Surely the face was very dark? And for some reason he appeared to be wearing an army uniform of sorts. The room, too, was . . . unexpected: it seemed to be upside down.

"Who are you?" the agent croaked.

"Colonel Ononu, Area Commandant of the Nya Nyerere," the foreman said. "More to the point, my friend: who are *you*? And why? And from where? And sent by whom, man?"

Of course, Solo thought. The room wasn't upside down at all: he was lying on his back – and yet there was no sense of anything hard, no sign of any floor beneath him. His wrists and ankles hurt like hell. And as the thought formed in his mind, he was astonished to see them in front of him, apparently sticking straight up in the air. He tried to bring them down, failed, saw the pole running between the thongs binding them – and all at once remembered: the deserted glade, the officer with the revolver, the empty Uranium 235 canister, the homing device that had been discovered and used to decoy him into an ambush. . . .

"I said who are you?" the chunky officer repeated.

"I might feel more inclined to reply in a less disadvantageous position," Solo replied.

"You are in as happy a position as spies ever are," the Colonel said. "Who are you?"

"I am not a spy. My name is Napoleon Solo. I am engaged on mineralogical research for . . . a certain government."

"You are an arab spy," the officer said levelly.

"Don't be ridiculous. How can I be an arab?"

Ononu slapped his face dispassionately. Pain flamed through the agent's body as the blow jarred his head. "How can you *not* be an arab?" the soldier sneered.

"I tell you I am a European – "

"Ridiculous. With those hands and fingers? With those teeth?"

"It was a disguise. They can be brought back to normal – "

"And you have even shaved off your beard – see, there's the outline where the skin is paler!"

Solo was silent. He must have acquired a deeper tan while he was with the caravan, and the removal of the false beard had showed it up. His disguise had been too clever: now it was backfiring on him. . . . "Who . . . what is the Nya Nyerere?" he asked at last.

"The liberation army of southwest Sudan."

"Well, it'll hardly recommend itself to *you* for its original purpose, but at least it will serve to identify me: there is a *laissez-passer* in the breast pocket of my shirt, vouching for my bona fides and signed by a high government official."

Fingers snatched the document from Solo's pocket. From his cramped position, he took in what he could of the room while it was being read. It seemed to be some sort of office, with filing cabinets, a desk, charts and maps on the wall. Through a window he could see a steep, tree-covered cliff and the corner of a red brick building. From somewhere outside shouted words of command drifted in. The pole under which he was slung rested between two banks of steel cabinets.

"This piece of paper is worthless," a second voice, which Solo had not heard before, said crisply behind him. A man in dark robes walked into his view. It was the stranger he had seen talking to Ahmed at Wadi Elmira and encountered again when he had made his abortive attempt to rejoin the caravan the next day.

"I have myself met Mr Solo," the man said contemptuously. "He is a Russian, fair-haired, and more slimly built than this man. . . . Did you imagine for one moment, my poor fool," he continued, gazing down at Solo, "that THRUSH would be so naive as to let your clumsy attempts at espionage go undetected? We have been on to you ever since you joined the caravan – only the precise identification of which man was the spy remained. And this you kindly supplied yourself when you tried to join up again after we left Wadi Elmira."

"And the Uranium 235?" Solo asked, playing for time.

"Was never with this caravan at all. When it was taken away from the first camel train between Casablanca and Alexandria, it was flown straight here by helicopter. Did you think we would be so foolish as to continue with the same system once we knew it had been discovered? Did you think your radio messages from the caravan went unnoticed? We merely let you play your little game so that you could be lured to a place more suitable for your . . . interrogation. You were *meant* to discover the canister and follow it . . ."

The agent said nothing. There was nothing to say.

"And now we come back to the question," the dark man said. "Who are you and who is employing you?"

Again, Solo remained silent.

"Very well," the dark man said at length. "As I had feared, we shall have to resort to less . . . polite methods . . . Colonel?"

Ononu moved back into Solo's field of vision. He picked up a telephone from the desk and barked a few words into it in a dialect the agent could not identify. Then, dropping the receiver back into its cradle, he walked over and stood looking down at the helpless man.

"Man, you got yourself into some trouble," he said. "Neither you nor your bosses, whoever they are, can do us any harm now: we're all set to go. . . . But there's a Council member arriving today, and he'll want all the ends tidied up before he comes. So we have to find out all about you just for the record. We like to know who we've beaten. . . . You'll talk, too, sooner or later. Everybody talks. But in your case it has to be sooner, see? Now why not save us a lot of trouble – and yourself, too – by telling us what we want to know?"

"I have already told you who I am," Solo said.

The Colonel shook his head. He flung out his arms and dropped them to his side again. "*I* don't know," he said. "I don't know."

There was a knock on the door. "Come in," the dark man called.

Footsteps crossed the floor behind Solo's head. "This spy will not say anything," Colonel Ononu said. "There's a Council member arriving at six. I want to know before then who he is – who he really is – and who sent him, and what's he doin' here anyway. Right? . . . You'd better take him away into the mountain . . ."

There was a short pause, and then, "It will be a pleasure," two voices said simultaneously, one in French and one in Arabic. Two large men moved across and took up the ends of the pole under which Solo was slung.

One was Ahmed; the other was the half-caste with the broken nose whom the agent had worsted in the fight in the alleyway at Casablanca.

*

"It would be much easier for everybody, old chap, if you'd just tell me all about it," General Mazzari said to Illya. They were sitting in a small office off the corridor leading to the cavern where the reactor was. Between them, a flat-topped desk was covered in papers. The walls were hung with what looked like production charts and graphs, and there was a plaster relief map of the Sudan and surrounding countries to one side of the door. Mazzari's Walther PPK, with its dull black barrel and brown grips, lay heavily among the papers by his hand.

"There's not much to tell, really," Kuryakin said. "I am afraid I must plead guilty to being inquisitive. I was trying to find my colleague Waverly – I told one of your colonels who stopped me about him – and I came across an airstrip and then a road. . . . Well, you can imagine how curious I was, finding a road and a runway in the middle of an unexplored forest . . ."

"Go on."

"Yes. Well, the next thing I discovered was a silo with a

missile in it. Not that I was prying, but I almost fell into it. It seems to me quite reasonable for anyone finding things like this to look around a bit."

"But I found you in here, old chap. In here. The place is closely guarded, you know. Very closely guarded."

"That was unintentional. I did not mean to come in here – indeed, I did not know of the existence of the place."

"Unintentional?"

"I was tired. A convoy of trucks passed me and I – well, I stole a lift; I swung aboard the back just as the last one passed me."

"Just as it passed you. I see. But you had a vehicle of your own."

"I had to leave it. There was a bridge down and I came on on foot."

"And what did you find inside this truck?"

"An unmarked crate – two crates, rather."

"Yes?"

"When the truck stopped, I waited for a minute and then I got out. I could see at once that I was in some place I had no business to be – so I thought I had better go. I was trying to find a way out when you . . . captured me."

Mazzari picked up the gun and examined it. "You have indeed stumbled upon something that does not concern you," he said at last. "But we are ready to strike within the next few days; in a week we shall be masters of the whole Sudan. Probably of the whole of Africa, old chap. Perhaps your unwelcome arrival does not matter so much – but I have a feeling . . . There is a highly placed official of the organization helping us who is due to arrive shortly. The decision must be his. I fear he may think you have learned more than is good for you. And even if your life should be spared, you will have to stay here as our . . . guest, shall we say? . . . until after we have acted."

"It sounds very intriguing."

"Intriguing! If only you knew, old chap! Do you realize how much work, how much planning, has gone into this scheme?"

"To build a redoubt like this must in itself have presented enormous difficulties," Illya encouraged him.

"But of course. There were the natural caverns to start with – we had the advantage of knowing about these. But our friends had to fly in vast quantities of materials undetected, instruct the labour force we provided and supervise the construction. . . . it was a fantastic task. For three years we have been slaving underground here. Three years. Because the place had to be invisible from the air, you see. The arabs have reconnaissance planes which frequently pass over Halakaz."

"There is certainly no sign of construction work on the surface – but what about the airstrip?"

"You would think it could be seen for miles, wouldn't you?" Mazzari was as boastful as a child with a new toy. "Undetectable. Not a sign. From the ground it looks like any runway, but we had the greatest camouflage expert in Europe . . . because there are no buildings, you see, skilful variations of tone and texture in the asphalt can blend it in perfectly with the surroundings."

"You have been very clever, General."

"Clever? That is only the beginning! We have a cyclotron – you probably saw the spiral tubes? – and we are building a synchrotron which will have an energy level of ten thousand million electron volts! That has to wait until we can enlarge the caverns still further, because the ring of tubing must be a hundred metres in diameter. In a year, we shall have completed a Fast Reactor using tamed Plutonium and liquid Sodium – and then we shall be able to dispense with the old-fashioned hydro-electric plant which always runs the risk of being detected by people exploring the falls. Then, too, we shall be our own masters at every stage of our weapons programme: at the moment, we have to rely on – er – outside sources for certain isotopes."

"You mention a strike in the near future. If all this is to help you vanquish your enemies in Khartoum, the . . . organization . . . helping you must be altruistic. What can it profit them?"

"The organization – it is called THRUSH – is an international body of scientists and economists. It is not composed of altruists, but it is always prepared to consider helping the underdog – if he has a good cause. Our cause *is* good, so they helped us. And of course, as you say, it is a two-way deal. In return we provide the labour and the place – the one place in the world where THRUSH scientists can continue with their valuable research undisturbed by the prying eyes of jealous rivals and unknown to the world's espionage corps."

Kuryakin began to say something, thought better of it, and sighed. If this somehow likeable patriot had not yet realized that his poor little six-thousand strong army, and his labour force of refugees from the destroyed villages, were merely dupes in THRUSH's insatiable plan for world domination, his awakening would come soon enough.

For the missiles whose sleek shapes he had seen in their silos were no local pieces of atomic artillery designed to obliterate Khartoum; they were IRBM's – intermediate range ballistic missiles capable of destroying Rome, Paris, London, Berlin and Vienna!

"Your own men are in charge of the despatch of the missiles I saw?" he asked.

"Well, no, old chap. At the moment THRUSH technicians look after them. We haven't yet acquired the know-how to man the computer room and the control dugouts. . . . But we are training, we are training. A branch of my forces is on a special course at Gabotomi, on the farther side of this plateau. And there are supplementary courses at various places round about, you know. An elementary course had a narrow escape yesterday when the accursed arabs sacked a village not far from here – purely by coincidence, I hope."

"General," Illya began, "there is something I ought to tell you . . ."

A telephone on Mazzari's desk shrilled him into silence. "Forgive me," the soldier said when he had listened for a few moments, made a comment in his native language, and replaced the instrument. "The Council member of whom I spoke has arrived. I must leave you for a while. There are, as you see, no windows, no other doors, no means of exit from this room. The door through which I leave is solid and will be double-locked. Also there will be two armed men on duty outside it. My advice to you, old chap, is to make yourself comfortable and sit tight until I return. . . ."

He went out and Illya heard the solid clunk of metal as the

tumblers of the lock fell home. A moment later, boots scraped on the floor of the corridor as the guards took up position outside.

*

Napoleon Solo was strapped naked to a ten-foot plank. His ankles were bound and attached to a ring at one end, and his arms, stretched above his head, were tied at the wrist and fastened to the other. The ends of the plank rested on a table top and a chair, so that his head was lower than his feet.

Helpless and undignified on his back in this position, he had endured the age-old water torture. It was quite simple and very effective. They had plugged his nostrils with cotton wool and wedged an iron ring into his mouth so that it was jammed open. Broken-nose had then draped a long strip of thin muslin over Solo's face and carefully, lovingly, poured water – gallons and gallons of water – into the open mouth through the cloth. With the head unable to turn because of his own arms on either side the victim can only get rid of the water by trying to swallow it – but before each mouthful is swallowed it is always replaced by another. And in the meantime the victim has to breathe; the tortured lungs heave and try to drag in the air, but the attempt only draws in water ... and with the water comes the muslin, which is remorselessly sucked in to the windpipe. In a very short time the victim, gagging and retching, is half drowned with the water in his lungs, and half choked with the cloth.

The only trouble was that Solo's iron will was sufficiently strong to allow himself to be choked into unconsciousness before the spasms became violent enough to give the cue to the torturers to remove the muslin and start again.

After this had happened three times, Ahmed – whose dirty-nailed fingers had been occupying themselves pinching and prodding and squeezing here and there to punctuate the water treatment – straightened up from the agent's body and growled: "This is no good, my friend. We shall never get anywhere this way. The *salaud* will just go on choking himself unconscious. And the Colonel said he wanted results – quickly. We must make him talk some other way."

Broken-nose put down the jerrican and attached radiator

hose he had been using to supply the water. "Very well," he said. "Let us see how he reacts to electricity, eh?"

"You must have been someone's star science pupil," Solo gasped.

Broken-nose snarled: "We learned a few lessons in Algeria about water and electricity, and the boys upstairs learned some things by keeping their ears and eyes open when the French exploded their atom bomb in the Sahara in 1960."

"Of course," Solo muttered to himself. "W equals mc^2 – I thought it was familiar..."

"What is he gabbling about?" Ahmed asked.

"A sum I saw on a blackboard. That's the French way of expressing the atomic equation. We – others, that is, express it as E equals mc^2. But don't worry yourself about it: it's far too intelligent for you."

The camel-master plunged his fist into Solo's unprotected midriff. Once again the world dissolved into a red mist.

When the agent came to, the two men were attaching lengths of wire to various parts of his body with miniature bulldog clips. "This will make your beautiful eyes open wider," Broken-nose grinned, feeling Solo stir. "We have a fine truck magneto handy – when we hitch up the wires and spin the armature, you'll have your own built-in central heating system! And we can make it as hot as you like, according to how fast we spin!"

"And if that doesn't make you talk," Ahmed put in, "we shall have to start taking bits away from you – because you've been a naughty boy! Sure you wouldn't like to change your mind and tell us all about it?"

Solo remained silent and they went out, presumably to fetch the magneto.

The room appeared to be carved from the solid rock. It had been quite a long walk from the settlement where he had seen Ononu, first between army-style huts, then along a narrow gorge, and finally through a cave to a succession of passages hollowed out of the mountain. By the time the torturers had laid down the pole with its helpless burden, they had been gasping with the effort.

It was very cold. Solo shuddered uncontrollably, listening

to the hoarse noise of his own breathing and the small sounds made by the wires festooning him as they shivered in turn. The clips bit painfully into the tender areas of his flesh – though he knew this was nothing to the bolts of agony which would shortly be searing through him at the direction of his torturers. He hoped he would be able to stand it long enough for unconsciousness to save him again. . . .

Fingers were busy now about the cords which bound his wrists. He closed his eyes, tensing his muscles for the assault of pain. But there was something amiss – the fingers were soft. A cloying, exotic perfume washed over him.

"You are very pretty like that," a voice hissed in his ear, "but I could admire you better in another place at another time. Come – do you wish to stay here until they return?"

Solo's arms were free. He brought them down to his sides and turned his head. Yemanja was crouched beside the plank, her eyes glittering at him over an arab veil.

"Yemanja!" he exclaimed. "What are you doing here? How did you get here?"

"Talk later," the girl said urgently, busy about the bonds around his ankles. "Unclip the wires. I saw you being carried through Gabotomi on a pole and I guessed they would be bringing you here."

Painfully, his limbs suffering agonies as the blood coursed back into the veins, Solo sat up and swung his feet to the ground. He took two steps towards his clothes, where they had been dropped in a corner, and almost fell. There was a thundering behind his eyes and his head was spinning. The girl darted across and snatched up shorts, shirt and money belt. "Quick!" she whispered, climbing on to a desk against one wall. "They will be back any minute."

In a daze, the agent watched as she reached over her head and pushed at a grating set high up in the rock. The grille swung away with a metallic scrape. A moment later the girl had pitched clothes and belt into the dark opening beyond and hauled herself up after them.

Solo climbed stiffly on to the desk and grasped the hands held out to aid him from the blackness. He made the climb with difficulty and lay gasping while Yemanja lowered the grating back into place. They were in a tunnel hollowed out of the rock. It was about three feet high and there was a moist breeze blowing from somewhere ahead.

"Air conditioning," the girl said. "Very modern.... Put your things on and follow me."

Solo wriggled into his shorts and shirt, buckled the belt around his waist, and crawled after her along the damp, rough floor. After a while, the passage joined another, wider tunnel and they were able to move along this at a crouch. Judging by the draughts that he felt from time to time about his legs, there were a number of subsidiary passages joining the main one. Distantly, from somewhere behind, he heard the muffled sound of voices raised in argument or protest. Presumably his absence had been discovered.

Presently he could detect a faint radiance ahead, and soon they were standing upright in a cave dimly lit by reflected light from a series of radiating galleries.

"Now we stop for a minute and talk," Yemanja said. "But quietly, for sound carries far in the rock."

"All right," Solo whispered. "For a start, answer me some questions, will you? What is this place? How did you get here? – and how do you know all about these passages?"

"Is the mountain headquarters of the Nya Nyerere. The caves and the passages have been secret retreat of my people for many hundreds of years – but now their friends from Europe have built many new things inside the mountain. Factories and bombs and places to make electricity. Aeroplanes come and bring many things for the building – but although my people help with the new things, they keep some secrets for themselves. The Europeans know nothing of these old passages which bring air to the rooms, for example."

"Yes, Yemanja – but how do *you* know all about them?"

"I was born in Gabotomi," the girl said. "My father was Assyrian but my mother was a Gabotomi woman. I lived here as a child – before it stopped being town and became military camp – and we had to come into the mountain sometimes to escape the arabs."

"What are you doing here now?"

"Ahmed brought me to entertain troops and workers

with some other girls. But I know more than others. See – I will show you all the factory parts..."

She took Solo by the hand and led him along one of the passages leading off the cave. As they went farther down the tunnel, the light grew brighter and a confusion of noises manifested itself. Solo could distinguish the humming of generators, voices, a truck engine revving, and a whole series of tappings and hammerings. Soon they were passing a row of grilles set low down in the rock, from which the light was coming. Through the metal gratings, he caught glimpses of offices, lecture rooms and stores with men in uniform busy about their tasks below.

"But surely THRU – the Europeans – must know about the grilles . . . they must know how the air comes to their offices?" Solo asked.

"Of course. They know *about* the tunnels. But they do not know they are big enough for people to walk in. Many of our own people, even, do not know this."

"Can all the gratings be moved like the one we escaped from?"

"No. Only that one. The others are cemented in place – but we left that one in case any of our own men were tortured and we wished to escape them. . . . Look! Now you can see. . . ."

They had come to a wider embrasure, set chest high in the limestone wall. The girl pushed Solo towards it and he peered down through the iron bars. The noise was deafening now, and as he saw the sources of the sounds, he uttered a whistle of astonishment.

Fifty feet below him was the floor of the huge cavern Illya Kuryakin had seen when he got out of the truck. Solo's trained eye took in at a glance the cyclotron, the hundred-foot steel sphere of the atom furnace with the swarm of men still working on it, the partially completed cooling tubes, the banks of dials with their winking pilot lights, and, far above, the movable cranes running on rails set in the roof of the cave. Fork-lift trucks were whining here and there among the army of workmen, and in the background he could see the sinister, fish-like shape of a rocket on a low loader. Behind it, double doors admitted to a further chamber –

each one carrying in red lettering the legend in Arabic, French and English:

> DANGER! RADIATION HAZARD BEYOND THIS POINT!
> *Entry forbidden to personnel not wearing protective clothing.*

Yemanja was pulling at his arm. "Come," she whispered. "There is more to see . . ."

She led the way through a maze of passages which continually branched and divided again, rising and falling in the rock. After about a quarter of a mile, Solo noticed that the limestone showing through the gloom was glistening with moisture and the air was appreciably colder. A faint roaring noise vibrated all around them. A few minutes later they were looking over the edge of a gallery in the rock at the giant turbines and generators of the power station.

"Yemanja," Solo called over the thunder of the conduits. "Why do you think these people are offering to help the Nya Nyerere? What is all this great factory for?"

"They say it is to vanquish the arab government in Khartoum," the girl replied, her lips close to the agent's ear. "But they speak with lying voices, I think."

"You are right. These are evil men. Your people are being made the dupes for a much larger conspiracy. As soon as the work is finished, the Europeans will have no further use for them. They will all be killed. The secret work of which I spoke is to try and foil this plan. Will you help me, Yemanja?"

"Am I not helping you already?" the girl said simply. "You are no longer in the interrogation room. That is why I show you all this."

"I am sorry. I am very grateful; I owe you much . . . but tell me one thing more. Will Ahmed and the other not guess that we escaped through the hinged grating and follow us? If they locked the door when they went out, there is no other way we could have gone."

The girl shrugged. "Perhaps. You were securely tied and they probably left the door unlocked. Even if not, if they did open the grating, they could never find their way through the passages, for Ahmed is not of our people and the other is a nothing. . . . Now – I will show you the rooms where the important ones, the chiefs of the organization, talk."

And once again she led Solo down a narrow tunnel in the rock...

*

Some time after Illya Kuryakin had been left alone in Mazzari's office, the General returned with two men – a short, squat army officer in uniform and a tall man in dark robes. The former was Colonel Ononu; the latter, the Russian saw to his intense surprise, was Hassan Hamid.

"Ah, Mr Kuryakin!" the soldier said. "I did warn you of the consequences of a too inquisitive lens, did I not?"

"The Council member will be with us in a few minutes," Mazzari said. "Until then the precise consequences of Mr Kuryakin's – er – transgression cannot be arrived at."

"What name did you say?" Hassan Hamid exclaimed. "But *this* is Solo – the man to whom those documents rightfully belong!"

"I have never seen this man before in my life," Kuryakin said, looking him straight in the eye.

"What kind of joke is this? Why, you came to see me in my villa at Khartoum. . . . I gave you the authorization myself. . . ."

Illya shook his head slowly, his eyes wide with innocence.

"I hardly think, Excellence," Ononu said awkwardly, "that it can be the same man. I myself saw this one, almost three days ago, in the desert of thorns – heading north in a Landrover."

"And I had seen him cross the southern border a day before that," Mazzari put in with a puzzled frown.

"But that is impossible. Absolutely impossible. He travelled here from Khartoum in the caravan with the decoy canister . . . or at least almost here. Colonel – you were with the caravan for the first two or three days: was there or was there not this spy among its members?"

"There was *a* spy – or so you told me," Ononu said slowly. "But the only evidence I saw was of the radio transmissions. By the time he was caught, I had already left the caravan two days. Whereas I do know that this man was three hundred and fifty miles to the southwest when the spy tried to rejoin the train after Wadi Elmira. . . . Also, I myself caught the man following the homing device: you yourself saw him earlier today."

"But the papers that man had were given – "

"The photograph on them was of the other man."

"I told you they must have been altered, forged, you fool!" Hamid said furiously. "Where is the man, the other one, now?"

"He is being interrogated, as you know."

"Come, then – we will soon get to the bottom of this foolishness." Hassan Hamid grasped Ononu roughly by the arm and stormed him from the room.

Illya smiled deprecatingly at Mazzari. "I was attempting to tell you, General," he said quietly, "that I fear you and your well-trained little army are being made into dupes. The organization THRUSH is making use of you to help build this arsenal – and when it is finished, you will be . . . dispensed with. I assure you they have no intention of using these weapons to help you take Khartoum or any other city in the Sudan."

"That is ridiculous, old chap."

"Are you a missile expert, General?"

"No. But . . ."

"Then how can you explain the fact that the weapons are not short-range missiles such as would be suitable for such a task, but intermediate range rockets capable of delivering atomic warheads all over Europe?"

"How can you know that? You are a photographer – "

"I must plead guilty to a little deception there, General. I am not at liberty to tell you for whom I work, but I *am* a missile expert – and what I tell you is the truth."

The Russian's even voice carried conviction, and for the first time Mazzari hesitated. "Moreover," the quiet voice continued, "if they were really going to help you conquer the arabs of the north, would there really be such a highly placed Khartoum official working for them?"

127

"A *Khartoum* official?"

"Hassan Hamid. Do you mean you didn't know? He's the head of – "

"I don't believe it," Mazzari said blankly. "It cannot be true."

"I can prove it to you. Now."

"I challenge you to do so, old chap."

Kuryakin unbuttoned his shirt and reached for the money belt around his waist. From one of the pouches at the back he produced the miniature tape recorder and a packet of photographs. "These pictures show him in his official reception office in Khartoum," he said. "You can see the arms, the crest, the flag flanking the wall map . . ."

While Mazzari stared in disbelief at the prints, the Russian started the tiny recorder. Faintly but distinctly Hamid's voice spoke:

"*. . . There are one or two cut-throat bands of renegade blacks . . . We Muslims of the north are continually being misrepresented by the backward negroes of the south. . . . Go tonight to the police station at this address. The necessary documents will be waiting for you. . . . There are various charges, payable to the departments. . . .*"

Illya switched the machine off. "It could be faked, of course," he said. "And so could the photos. But, taking it together with the strange confusion that appears to exist about some document signed by Hamid, I think you must agree that my warning should at least be carefully considered."

Mazzari was still sitting thunderstruck at his desk when the door burst open and Ononu returned with Hassan Hamid. The arab's face was dark with anger, and Ononu looked perplexed. "The man's gone; he has apparently escaped," he exclaimed, snatching off his beret and slashing his thigh with it. "I don't understand how it can have happened!"

A telephone was ringing on the desk. Mazzari picked it up and listened for a moment. "All right," he said absently. "We are all here."

He looked up as he replaced the receiver. "The Council member is on his way in," he announced. "Perhaps he will be able to answer a few questions that badly need a reply."

The door opened again and the three of them stood stiffly and bowed to the young man who came in.

It was Rodney Marshel.

CHAPTER FIFTEEN

A LADY TO THE RESCUE!

"*Marshel!*" Illya was on his feet, his mouth open in astonishment. "Surely, it can't be . . . surely you are not . . ."

"Yes, Kuryakin – I am a member of the Council of THRUSH," the young man snapped, very different now from the languid, diffident person they had seen in Khartoum. "Waverly and your poor organization don't have a chance: we have agents everywhere; we were on to you from the moment you landed in Casablanca."

"It seems to have taken you quite a time to catch up with us, in that case," Illya said mildly. "Now I understand why there was no helicopter when I arrived in Stanleyville. You didn't pass on any of the messages."

"Of course not," Marshel said contemptuously. "Neither yours nor any of the ones Solo so laboriously transmitted from the caravan. So far as Waverly is concerned, the last we heard from you was in Alexandria."

"And of course you knew we were coming because Waverly *had* in fact tipped you off?"

"Quite. The only remotely clever thing you did, actually, was to conceal from me the fact that you were seeing this fool Hamid when you went out from the hotel. And when I *had* found out, the fact that you had switched roles, as it were, caused us a certain amount of trouble. . . . As for you, you bungling oaf," he continued, turning to glare coldly at Hamid himself, "your duplicity might have imperilled the whole operation."

The man had gone a sickly grey colour. "I . . . I don't know what you mean," he stammered. "My instructions were that there would be a spy travelling with the caravan; that I was to try and identify him; but that he was to be permitted to find and follow the decoy canister. I carried them out. It was not my fault that – "

"I'm not talking about the caravan. Was it part of your instructions to receive the spy in your own house and issue

130

him with a *laissez-passer* so that you could line your own dirty pocket?"

"But I didn't," Hamid cried. "I keep telling everybody – *this* is the man who came to see me. He is a Russian government mineralogist. I saw no connection with the caravan; it was part of my normal cover activity – "

"*You* saw," Marshel grated. "Like all politicians, you saw only the chance to feather your own nest – and you took it without any heed of the consequences. You didn't check – and that's not Solo but Kuryakin!"

"I swear I – "

"How many times do I have to say it? THRUSH requires absolute and complete loyalty from its members at all times. At all times. The interests of THRUSH must come before everything else, always. You have transgressed against this law; now you will have to pay."

Hassan Hamid was on his knees, the fine bones of his swarthy face outlined in a dew of sweat. "No!" he cried. "No, no. I beg of you . . ."

Marshel had drawn a small Beretta automatic from his pocket. Cooly, he sighted along the barrel at the pleading figure and squeezed the trigger. As the little gun spat flame, Hassan Hamid jerked back on to his heels, staring in disbelief at the blood spurting between fingers which had flown instinctively to cover his chest. Marshel fired again and Hamid crashed over on to his back. He tried to sit up, groaned and sank to the floor again.

The man from THRUSH pumped six more shots into the body twitching under the scarlet-stained robes. When at last the convulsive movements had stopped, he drew another clip of ammunition from his pocket and calmly reloaded the gun. "Now – are there any questions?" he asked.

Mazzari, Ononu and Illya were still staring aghast at the murdered man.

"All right," Marshel continued. "Now you, Kuryakin. Although I naturally know a lot about Waverly's organization, there must be a lot more that such highly placed Enforcements Agents as Solo and yourself can tell me. Before you die, you will tell me these things – that is why you have been . . . encouraged . . . to find your way here, where we can question you at leisure. Your deaths will be slow, too, for you have caused us much trouble."

"Just a minute, old chap." Mazzari was on his feet, a frown creasing his brow. "Am I to understand, then, that this man" – he gestured at the body on the floor – "was in fact a Khartoum official, after all?"

"Of course he was. How do you think caravans composed mainly of arab mercenaries were able time and time again to pass through the country unquestioned? And who do you imagine provided the escorts which brought them as far as the edge of the forest?"

"But in view of the Plan, old chap, surely it would have been – "

"The Plan! Are you really naive enough to imagine that an organization such as ours would really go to all this trouble just to help a handful of self-seeking guerilas? Be your age – General. Your use is at an end, now that our own plans are virtually completed . . . And don't call me Old Chap."

Faced with the ruin of his hopes in a single sentence, Mazzari behaved with restraint. Compressing his lips, he exchanged a glance with Ononu and sat quietly down again.

"I do not see how the information you say we can give you will help," Illya said, playing for time. Solo was somewhere in the underground complex under interrogation, he knew, and he had to make up his mind what to do.

"As I was saying before this jumped-up boy interrupted me," Marshel replied, "the info. I want from you – "

"*I say! Hardly the way for a jolly old Englishman to talk, what!*" Astoundingly, the voice – with its exaggerated mimicry of Marshel's accent – was Solo's own. It seemed to come from the air. The four men in the room swung round in astonishment. No other person had come in. For once, Marshel was at a loss. "What – what – Solo! What's that? Where are you?" he mouthed.

"*I said that's hardly the way for an Englishman to talk,*" Solo's normal voice repeated.

Marshel's eyes glinted. "I'm not an Englishman," he snapped in spite of himself.

"*Ah, that accounts for it, then. I thought all that frightfully frightful and doocidly top-hole stuff was laid on a bit too thick...*"

"The grating!" Ononu cried suddenly in a reflex, realizing where the voice came from. In the same instant Marshel, his face black with fury, loosed off a burst of fire at the grille set high in the wall.

They all simultaneously realized the danger. As the bullets spanged off the metal cover and ricocheted with shrill screams around the room, they hurled themselves to the floor.

Illya was the first to recover. His cameras and field-glasses were on Mazzari's desk, where the General had put them when they came in, and he had been waiting for just such an opportunity. Snatching up the binoculars by the strap, he scythed the heavy case across the desk top and swept the Walther to the ground as he retrieved the gun-camera in his other hand. Marshel was already aiming the Beretta at him as he pressed the release, still holding the device at his waist.

It was a lucky shot. Before the man could fire, the tiny nickel-jacketed bullet struck the automatic half way along the barrel and spun it from his hand. Marshel snatched his hand back as though it had been scalded, shaking the fingers to ease the tingling. Mazzari, in the meantime, had placidly regained his seat. He made no move to pick up the Walther ... or to aid Ononu, who had apparently been hit by a ricochet and was now sitting on the floor clutching one shoulder.

But the THRUSH man could move fast too. Before Illya had recovered from the success of his snap shot, he was through the door and pounding away down the corridor towards the caverns.

"General," the Russian said urgently. "Are you on our side?"

"I am afraid I seem to have no side left to be on, old chap," Mazzari said sadly. "From now on you had better regard us as neutral...."

"Right," Kuryakin said. "Solo? ... Can you find your way to the big cave where the reactor is?"

"*Yes – or at least I have a guide who can,*" Solo's voice replied through the grating.

"Good. Make your way there and we'll join forces. I have five shots left in the gun-camera. Marshel's Beretta is buckled and useless. But there's" – he paused and looked enquiringly at Mazzari, who stared impassively back at him – "there's the Walther," Kuryakin continued, scooping the heavy gun up from the floor. "And I'll see if Hamid was armed. . . . No, he wasn't. Well, we'll have to win what we can from the other side. See you there."

"Okay," Solo called. "We're on our way!"

As Illya left the office, Mazzari was pressing down a switch and starting to speak into a desk microphone in front of him.

"*This is Mazzari,*" he heard the voice boom from P-A speakers all over the redoubt as he hurried towards the door leading to the caverns. "*This is a message to all Nya Nyerere personnel. There are two groups of Europeans at large in the fortress – our so-called allies and another. There may be fighting between them. You are not – repeat not – to take any part whatever in this conflict. Stop all work immediately and proceed to Gabotomi. Retain your arms but take no part in the fighting. Do not use them unless anyone tries to requisition them. If they do, you may defend yourselves. . . . I repeat: stop all work immediately and proceed to Gabotomi.*"

Illya opened the steel door cautiously and peered around it at floor level. Marshel must know he would follow and might be waiting to pick him off with a colleague's gun as he came through. But no burst of fire greeted the opening door, and he slipped quietly into the cavern and surveyed the scene from behind the line of parked trucks.

African workmen were already streaming from the cave containing the partially completed atomic plant, heading for a pair of double doors set in the far rock face. Among them were several groups of soldiers, their rifles slung. The sounds of hammering had stopped, the trucks were silent, and the only noise to be heard over the shuffle of feet was the descending whine of the generators as they spun to a standstill.

When two-thirds of the labour force had vanished through the double doors, Marshel and about a dozen Europeans appeared on a steel gallery outside a glass-fronted control office half way up the cavern wall.

"*Stop!*" Marshel shouted. "Get back to your work, damn you. Go back at once to the machines where you belong!"

The file of Africans below looked up impassively and continued to stream through the doors.

"Get back, I say," Marshel screamed, "or we shall start shooting to show who's master here."

The soldiers and workers went on walking quietly out.

"All right, then – you've asked for it!" the man from THRUSH yelled. A ragged burst of fire crackled from the miscellany of pistols and automatics wielded by the men on the gallery. The crowd beneath surged and wavered. There were figures lying on the ground. But as the majority pressed forwards towards the doors, the soldiers among them wheeled smartly out, unslung their rifles and sank to their knees in the firing position. Their first volley crashed out as Marshel's men began firing for the second time.

The Europeans abruptly withdrew from the gallery, leaving three men slumped over the steel rail. The soldiers waited a moment, and then shepherded the rest of the workers out, dragging the dead and wounded with them. In a few moments the place was deserted.

Kuryakin hesitated. During the firing, he had slipped out from behind the trucks and made his way into the centre of the vast floor. Now he was sheltering behind an abandoned fork-lift. But his problem – and Solo's when he appeared – was different from Marshel's: to the THRUSH man, it was simply a matter of rounding up two interlopers and then trying to get on good terms with the workers again, whereas to them, with their limited amount of fire-power, it was a question of tactics; of getting the opposition to show itself and eliminating it member by member....

A low murmur of voices which had been coming from the control room now grew louder as Marshel and the THRUSH technicians came out and climbed down the stairs from the gallery to the ground. "Remember," he was saying as they fanned out over the floor, "there are only two of them. They don't know the layout of the place and I don't think they've linked up yet. One of them is armed; the other isn't. Shoot to kill – but if you can bag 'em alive, so much the better."

"Any special order we should search in, sir?" one of the men asked.

"Yes. You, Manson and Trottman take the passage and the power station. I'll take Ahmed and Fawzi and search the reactor cavern, and the other three can look around in here.... And if those musical-comedy characters in uniform show their noses out of their office, shoot them too."

Kuryakin shifted silently round to keep the truck between himself and the searchers as they separated. Marshel, Ahmed and Fawzi – the broken-nosed man – disappeared through the opening towards the reactor, while three other men went through the door leading to Mazzari's office and the hydro-electric plant. The agent was just wondering how best to deal with the trio left in his own section when his eye caught a blur of movement on the far side of the cave.

Napoleon Solo was dropping from an opening in the rock on to one of the searchers.

He landed on the man's shoulders and sent him sprawling, twisting the gun from his grasp as he fell. Before they were up, the other two had spun round, pistols at the ready. Illya dropped one with the Walther, but the other fired simultaneously with the roar of Solo's borrowed gun. Both shots went home: the THRUSH gunman slumped to the floor – and the slug meant for Solo slammed into the back of the man he had jumped on, just as he was rising to close with the agent.

"Three down and six to go!" Solo yelled. "Nice to see you, Illya! Stay there and cover me while I try and get the guns from the dead ones up in the gallery...."

Footsteps clattered towards them from the other cavern as Solo sprinted for the stairs. The Walther PPK boomed deafeningly as Illya fired in support. Marshel, Ahmed and Fawzi withdrew hurriedly around the corner of the archway.

"Any luck?" the Russian called. Solo's head appeared over the balcony railing. It shook slowly from side to side. "They'd already thought of it and lifted them," he said. "*Look out! Behind you...*"

Kuryakin whirled and flung himself flat behind the fork-lift truck as a fusillade of shots erupted from among the line of parked lorries. The three men had returned from the power station....

He emptied the Walther and began firing the camera-gun, although the range was really too extreme for the tiny weapon. Two of the men were already sprawled on the ground between the heavy wheels but bullets from the third were striking sparks from the steel frame of the fork-lift, uncomfortably close to his head. He couldn't see where the man was hidden – and then suddenly a final shot from Solo's gun, which had been firing sporadically in his support, flushed him out. He careened sideways from the cab of one of the army trucks, scrabbled futilely at the starred windscreen, and plunged to the rock floor.

Illya rose to his feet and looked back at Solo. The agent held up his gun and gestured to show that his ammunition was exhausted. At this moment the sudden silence was shivered by a woman's scream, shrill and terrified. It came from somewhere behind Solo, through the control room. . . .

He turned and dashed past the banks of meters, gauges and dials to find himself in a long corridor. Ahmed – who had obviously been sent to outflank him – was standing over Yemanja. The girl was lying in a tumble of robes on the floor, with blood trickling from a corner of her mouth.

"You dirty little slut," the big man shouted. "I'll teach you to meddle in affairs that don't concern you and help spies to escape!" He hauled the girl to her feet and chopped at her face viciously with the back of his hand.

Solo landed on his back like a tiger, his right arm feeling for a judo lock under the man's chin. Ahmed twisted and dropped to the floor, dragging the agent with him. Locked together, pummelling and gouging, they rolled down the passage and back into the control room. Solo managed to free one arm and caught the camel-master with two uppercuts to the jaw, but the blows hardly seemed to shake him.

He rose up on to his knees, his arms at full stretch, and closed his great hands inexorably around Solo's windpipe. The agent threshed and writhed on the floor, his hands tearing at the sinewy wrists, his feet and knees seeking a purchase. But the thumbs pressing into his throat would not relax their iron grip and the thundering in Solo's ears threatened to engulf the world.

There was a whining of hydraulic rams, and Illya Kuryakin

rose slowly into view over the rail of the gallery, seated on the fork-lift of the truck. The viewfinder of the small camera held to his eye spat once, and the pressure on Solo's throat relaxed. Ahmed gave a strange coughing groan and collapsed, a dead-weight across his body.

Kuryakin strode through and helped the sobbing girl to her feet, rolled the body of the camel-master off Solo, and said crisply: "That was my last shot, Napoleon. We haven't a round between us. What do we do now?"

"I should say that was an academic question," the voice of Rodney Marshel said levelly behind them. "Get down those stairs, the three of you – and move!" He was standing with Fawzi at the gallery entrance to the control room. With a gesture of resignation, Solo led the way past the two steadily held automatics and began to descend the staircase. Yemanja and Illya followed.

They had gone down three or four steps when two shots so close that they sounded like a single explosion thundered in the cavern. Fawzi and Marshel were flung forward and hurled on top of the others, so that all five of them tumbled down the remainder of the staircase in one tangled heap.

Illya was the first on his feet. Far across the floor of the cavern, booted and gleaming at the foot of the ramp leading to the entrance tunnels and the open air, he saw the figure of Rosa Harsch, wreathed in the smoke which still curled from the barrel of the automatic rifle in her hands.

*

"You know what you have to do, Illya?" Napoleon Solo asked hoarsely, massaging his bruised throat with one hand.

The Russian nodded. "I shall need a great deal of wire and an alarm clock," he said. "Detonators I can probably raise from one of the many stores here."

"Okay. Off you go then. We'll see you later. . . . General, I'm sorry, but I hope you understand why we have to do this."

Mazzari retained his dignity in defeat. Still supporting a grey-faced Ononu – who had lost quite a lot of blood through the ricochet which had torn his shoulder – he nodded in

138

turn. "I suppose so, old chap," he said wearily. "To be honest, we couldn't use any of them on our own, anyway."

"It's probably just as well. I'm afraid we cannot offer to help you in any way in the furtherance of your – er – private war. Now tell me, apart from your own troops, are there any refugees in the forest in this area?"

"None. We have rigorously excluded them from an area twenty miles in radius, of which this of course is the centre."

"Fine. I will give you three hours to clear every man, woman and child of your own people – plus such equipment as you consider necessary – from the same area. I regret very much the destruction of Gabotomi, but it cannot be avoided. . . . I suggest you take one of the trucks. Oh – and I believe this is yours?" He picked up the empty Walther and handed it to Mazzari.

The soldier was almost in tears. He took the gun, slammed it into its holster, snapped his cane under his arm, saluted, and helped Ononu away towards the line of trucks.

"What time shall I set this for?" Kuryakin asked later, looking up from an old-fashioned alarm clock in a nest of terminals, wires and junctions. The truck which was to take them away was waiting with its engine running, and the four of them were gathered in the control room.

"Make it three hours from now," Solo said. "And I hope you can find your way back to that Landrover in the dark!"

"I'm not worried about that," the Russian said. "What I cannot understand is Miss Harsch's part in all this."

Rosa Harsch smiled. "I work for the German government at Bonn," she said huskily. "We are naturally somewhat sensitive about others obtaining nuclear weapons – and we like to keep a close eye on anybody who may seem to be doing so illegally. . . . But I thought you were not quite what you seemed either, my friend. Maybe each of us recognizes his own kind!"

She raised a blonde eyebrow and held his gaze with a meaning look.

CHAPTER SIXTEEN

INVITATION TO THE DANCE

"IT was fortunate," Alexander Waverly said in his office some days later, "that this fellow Mazzari was sufficiently persuaded by your evidence to withdraw his chaps from the fray. Whichever side he had been on, it would have been deuced awkward for us: it's no part of the Command's duty to interfere in civil disputes in any country."

"Yes, I thought of that afterwards," Illya Kuryakin said. "If he *had* thrown in his lot with us, we could have been accused of working against the lawful government of the Sudan; and if he'd fought against us, those on the other side would have made out that we were helping to suppress a minority! You can't win in a situation like that ... !"

"No repercussions on the – er – end-product?" Napoleon Solo asked.

Waverly tossed a morning paper across the huge desk towards him and felt in his pocket for a pipe.

"EARTHQUAKE IN THE SOUTHERN SUDAN?" Solo read half way down the front page. "*Seismographs as far apart as Santa Barbara, Tokio and Edinburgh registered shock-waves the day before yesterday whose epicentre was placed in an unexplored region of the Southern Sudan. The shock, which was of short duration, is thought to have been an earth tremor, although certain characteristics showed points in common with large man-made explosions, experts said. The Sudan government last night accused rebel factions in the southwest of having caused the explosion. A communique issued by the so-called 'Nya Nyerere' laid the blame squarely on 'government elements', however. . . . There have been no reports of casualties in the area. . . .*"

"Yes," Solo said reflectively, laying the paper down. "Best to leave it at that, I suppose...."

"You gentlemen are lucky that the human character is so fallible," Waverly continued, reaching for his tobacco pouch. "If Hassan Hamid had not been greedy enough to want to line his own pocket – and if Marshel hadn't been such an egomaniac that he thought he could decoy you to his headquarters and wrest our secrets from you – you might well have been murdered with the man Mahmoud in Alexandria."

"What about Marshel's own secrets," Illya asked. "Do *we* have those?"

"Oh, yes. The Eros newsagency was a THRUSH satrap, as you suspected. Our people found complete lists of the scientists and technicians responsible for stealing the Uranium 235 in Marshel's office safe. The CIA are getting on to their opposite numbers to have them all winkled out. . . . Good God! I seem to have run out of tobacco!" He stared unbelievingly at the empty pouch.

For an instant it trembled on Solo's lips to point out that there must have been several ounces deployed around the room in the selection of unsmoked pipes littering ashtrays, desk and occasional tables. Then he thought better of it and said quietly: "I'll see that some is sent in to you, sir, on my way out." It was, after all, a good thing that human nature was so fallible. . . .

"To be sure, to be sure," Waverly was saying. "You gentlemen are due for a few days leave, are you not? Just how do you propose to spend it?"

"So far as I am concerned," Kuryakin said with a rare smile, "I have first to search my mind for a really good reason to refuse a pressing invitation to visit Dusseldorf!"

Solo grinned. "I'm staying home," he said. "There's a lot of attractions I've missed in New York lately. Tonight, for example, I've got a ticket for a first-night at El Morocco – they tell me the new middle-eastern belly dancer there is *sensational* . . . !"

The Man from U.N.C.L.E. No. 5
The Finger in the Sky Affair

by

Peter Leslie

Five major air crashes in two months – the cause of all of them a complete mystery. In each case the plane's instruments were working perfectly, the crew was in command and ground-control in contact. Then the craft would suddenly nose-dive into the runway as it came in to land, killing most of the passengers. Those who weren't killed outright die mysterious deaths shortly after.

The men from U.N.C.L.E. make a dash from New York to Nice to track down the THRUSH agents behind the monstrous master-plan that is gradually becoming clearer. But not before Illya Kuryakin and Napoleon Solo are betrayed by the ones they trust and nearly annihilated by a desperate enemy....

SOUVENIR PRESS/FOUR SQUARE EDITION 3s. 6d.